IMPOSSIBLE PRINCESS

KEVIN KILLIAN

City Lights Books • San Francisco, California

Cover design: Jeff Mellin www.bigblueox.net

"Zoo Story" appeared in *Little Men* (Hard Press 1996)
"Spurt," "Ricky's Romance," "Hot Lights," and "White Rose"
appeared in *I Cry Like a Baby* (Painted Leaf 2001)

Library of Congress Cataloging-in-Publication Data
Killian, Kevin.
Impossible princess / Kevin Killian.
    p. cm.
ISBN 978-0-87286-528-0
1. Gays—Fiction. 2. Gays' writings, American. I. Title.

PS3561.I375I6 2009
813'.54—dc22

                              2009023361

Visit our website: www.citylights.com

City Lights Books are published at the City Lights Bookstore,
261 Columbus Avenue, San Francisco, CA 94133

IMPOSSIBLE PRINCESS

CONTENTS

YOUNG HANK WILLIAMS

with Derek McCormack

I never quit crying.

Mama wrapped me in a blanket. Me, a month old. September. We lit out toward dark.

Folks on horses. And in buggies. We walked. Stepping over shit. Beyond us, cottonfields. Full of hookworm.

Torches burned. Cotton wound around broomsticks. At a booth Mama bought a ticket. She sat me down. I cried. The seat was a plank. On crates. In a field.

A curtain covered a stage. In front, a table piled with blankets and joke books and pots and the like. A man come out. He juggled. Another man come out. He had a doll he made talk. The night smelled like guano. Bats black as blindfolds.

A woman up next. She had on tights. She stuck her hand in a drum. Drew out a ticket. Whoop went the man behind us. He won a French fan. He give it to Ma. She swatted. Flies hung like a net around me. Greenbottles.

The curtain split. A floodlight come on. The Professor appeared. He was old. He had everything silver—beard, fob, cane head. "And when you are dying," he said, "when you are drawing your last breath, who among you can say that you are prepared to meet the Angel of Death?"

At the lip of the stage he placed a skull, a trumpet, a Bible. "Because within each one of you, right this minute and every minute of your lives, resides Death. Death is within you. Death is your tenant. Death is the worm.

"Death grows fat in your intestines. Death is the animal in your blood. Death is the abscess overtaking your stomach wall. Death is the germ hiding in the alveoli of your lung. Right now. As we speak. In you and in you and in you—Death has found a home."

"It's home!" shouted a woman. Her leg lame.

He brought her onstage. "Mere years ago this affliction might've killed you. But now we have a cure."

He held up a bottle of his tonic. Egyptian Rooto-Bark Tonic. He rubbed a rag on her leg. "I can walk!" the lame lady said. He rubbed some on a deaf man's ears. "I can hear!" the deaf man said.

An old man bounded up. Jaw wrapped.

"You won't feel a thing." The Professor give him a swig, then shoved a plier in his mouth. "Get behind thee!" he said, holding up a molar. It was black and white.

The crowd clapped. Mama rose up. "He's got a bump on his back." At the base of my spine. A hot strawberry.

The Professor fingered it.

I wailed. The spotlight calcium.

"I tried everything," Mama said. "A poultice. A lance."

"Arachnids," the Professor said. "This baby has been

bitten by arachnids. They may now be nesting under his skin. They may be feeding on his blood. They may be readying to tumble out, hundreds of baby arachnids. Arachnids, my friends. Otherwise known as spiders."

The Professor raised me up over his head. His other hand raised up a bottle.

A piss-stream of tonic down my throat.

Four ladies danced onto stage, two and two like the Bible. One pair, dressed like nurses in white starchy cotton, swept my mother away to comfort her. Another pair in Oriental snake-charmer harem pants hustled me backstage in a cobra-like basket. Backstage, I was confronted by a silent row of babies, staring at me, all sizes from newborn to toddler, mostly dressed like me in flannel diaper made out of old cheesecloth and the like. These babies, held in women's arms silently, all meeting my stare with insolence.

The Professor's wife snapped her fingers while onstage her husband voiced the virtues of Egyptian Rooto-Bark Tonic and my mother gaped. Wife says, "That one will do," pointing to a baby that kind of looked like me. Strong hands pried open his diaper and filled it with spiders, whether real or toy I cannot say. Then the baby was paraded out on the wood stage again, a little senior to me, but one baby looks mighty like another don't they when they's crying. Even my own mother looked convinced, her mouth a raw "O" like an onion. I stood behind the curtain, tears dripping down my eyes. She held "me" in her arms while I looked on in undisguised envy.

That other boy, in the spotlight, and me, held back behind the curtain with faceless nobody women and babies. That other boy who, at the right moment of Professor's peroration, had his diaper dramatically lowered and a host of black spiders wriggled out of his ass and onto the wooden stage to shrieks.

Over my mother's shoulder he jeered my way, thumb to his nose, fingers wiggling.

Meanwhile a passionate lady with a camera was urging the women backstage to look statuesque, and for all the little children to bury their heads into their mother's sternums. She was passing around her business card and her credentials from the WPA. "You women are just one step away from the Dust Bowl Trail," she said. "You're migrant workers, minus the migrating."

"Geese migrate," spat one hard-faced bully.

"I agree," said Dorothea Lange more heartily, digging deep into her pocket and finding some quarters there. "Now watch the birdie."

With a quiet boom her camera exploded into light, we all froze in a stoic way. Offstage more applause, the Professor winding up his speech and the snake-charmer girls wafting into the audience with trays of Egypto Tonic, selling like crazy. The little boy who was playing "me" twinkled and shone like a diamond. I hated him, little upstart. My mother didn't know the difference—she, too, blinded by the spotlight.

The man who made the doll talk sat me on one knee and the doll on the other. I looked at the doll, and the doll looked back at me, first time I ever saw a mirror. The two nurses snuck behind me, marked my tailbone with a red heart and a red "X" to show where the wound had been. Course it was still there but felt smaller somehow. Impostor boy came off the stage, and they shoved me on the stage, happy in my mother's loving arms. At least—I looked happy. I was only a month old but already I had learned a passel of valuable lessons. Number one, there will always be somebody who can do your job better than you can. Number two, women can't be trusted. Number three, even a doll can have a personality that'll make people grin. Number four, you want to go out and knock them dead.

TOO FAR

with Thom Wolf

keeekeeekeeekeeekpittarumbapittarumbakkeeekeekeeek here the bassline keeps popping and drilling into Alan's feet through the club's concrete floor, it hurts to keep still, a positive force for evil he's thinking, or would be thinking if any room remained in his brain for thought but not while the DJ, a dark dervish ensconced in a booth high above the thrashing crowd, is waving his muscular arms and dropping needles, remixing, sweat pouring off him in waves. The lights focused on the DJ's hands, one after another on a row of spinning turntables, a ring on one finger flashes a turquoise glint, Alan can't see what he's wearing, just the bare sleek arms and the fingers, nimbler than eyesight, and the spine-pounding repetitive dancebeat *keeekeeekeeekeeek*, like Bernard Herrmann ripping the shower curtain down on Janet Leigh in *Psycho*. The boys on the dance floor go wild, mouths twisting in a quasi-sexual pain, eyes rolling back in their heads under beam after beam of white light that plays on their faces for a moment only, then darts elsewhere. It hurts to stand still but Alan doesn't trust himself to let go, to dance. He lowers his eyelids and feels that *Psycho* screech rip right through the sturdy soles of his shoes, plowing at Concorde speed through the muscles and veins in his legs right into the base of his spine. And that means danger, don't it Alan, base of spine is not a safe place for you.

Can he see you? Magisterial DJ high in his wooden booth, to him you must be a blip down here on the dance floor, one dot in a sea of writhing bodies. Can he see you standing frozen here like a ninny, afraid to dance? *I've got jet lag*, Alan remembers, soothed by this plausible excuse. The balm of the alibi. It had been a long 36 hours since alighting from Heathrow and *I'm not used to driving on the wrong side of the road* and *all the new people* and their *clipped accents* and the *different market conditions*. England was so different than the States and yet it isn't, he is finding, exactly like the Austin Powers pictures either. Apparently there are only maybe, three or four full-size pools, swimming pools, in all of County Durham. So where's the glamour? Nor is England like the sweet dusky glen he's conjured up after years of listening to UK pop music at home on his stereo. Boyband music for the most part crossed with massive doses of Kylie Minogue. Where did they film Nick Cave's video for "Where the Wild Roses Grow?" in which Kylie appears, drenched, in water ten inches deep, looking like a corpse, Nick Cave leaving roses on her face like Ophelia? Probably in Australia and yet, that glade, that eerie green darkness, is how he has always pictured England. Here in this club Alan's supremely unconfident, older and younger at the same time than the rest of the patrons. He's wearing a shirt for one thing. Subdued black T-shirt, fitted jeans. Where are the women? He's straight for another thing. Well, sort of.

Alan's 31 years old and lives in Greenbelt, Maryland, a suburb of D.C., in a small house he owns on a busy street near downtown, or what passes for downtown nowadays. It's near a Starbucks, which is the same thing. These guys all look high and it ain't coffee fueling their acrobatics. It's something stronger, in fact you can smell it, a thin high smell like kerosene or the cellophane his suits come back wrapped in from the laundry. Ecstasy? Is this what Ecstasy smells like?

At the office he keeps a photo of Kylie in a lurid pink swimsuit on his desk, his ideal girl, he jokes, and the reason his fiancée left him finally after a futile courtship of several years. She still lives in Greenbelt and their paths cross over and over. Vengeful bitch who's told everyone at the gym he never slept with her, not that it matters, who'd listen to a demented harpy who's presently, or so it appears, dating a black dude whose ass is bigger than hers? Since the breakup Alan's decided to make some changes in his life, get out of the rut all that dating had thrust him into. With his new chic haircut he looks pretty good to himself in the mirror. Thought of installing a full-length type mirror in his room so he could admire his body more, but then thought it was too gay. As it is, he must sidle up very close to the mirror and look way down, craning backwards, to check on his ass's perfection, in jockstrap, in gym shorts, rolled down perhaps so he can see the crack in his butt, its very beginnings where the hair trails between his cheeks, he can see his mole, like a tiny brown button of desire. When he does this a hot flash colors his skin, from his brow and temples right down to his groin. He steps away from the mirror with the guilt of one who has seen something forbidden.

That's why he doesn't keep any pets, they might spy him at the mirror sometime and think he was pretty weird.

A shirtless man moves in, takes his hand out of his belt. "A drink, mate?" he hears the man bellowing at him. He shakes his head ruefully, no thanks. Doesn't drink much, afraid of drinking, afraid of blackouts, father a drunk, mother a heavy drinker. The guy moves away, Alan dismisses him, another queer probably. What time is it? At home he'd be running, or down at the local gym. His hobbies include reenacting Civil War battles with former University mates—the good ol' days.

Alan's a white man of 6 foot 1, 180 lbs, dark brown eyes that look black at night, with broad shoulders and somewhat a heavy neck. He has a mole below his belt line, pretty much right at the small of his back. When he's worried he presses it, as though for good luck. His hair is thick and black, almost Latin; were the mole on his face he'd look like Enrique Iglesias, and his body is lightly hairy, his pubic hair the color of Coca-Cola. His hands and feet are large as well, so he feels constantly clumsy, but this endears him to people, that he's not as coordinated, that he's awkward. He likes things neat and tidy, a reaction to the sloppy house-keeping of his tipsy mother, and the chaotic conditions of former roommates.

Same man's back again, his shirt on this time. "You didn't say what you wanted," he yells. "So—here, cheers."

Alan nods, takes the warm glass, smiles politely, as though they were two strangers on a bus queue, then looks again up at the DJ booth. DJ's pale hand fluttering like an exotic bird across the spinning vinyl. The man's foot is next to his, planted squarely up against his boot. Same smell slides off Englishman—thin, greasy smell of brain cells all dizzy with Ecstasy. "New to town?"

Swimming pool chiefs have sent him to England to a big convention here in Durham, hands across the water, get it? Meet his Euro counterparts. The guys who get out there and deal and make it happen. You've got a half acre of ground, dig it. New passport—his first—new David Beckham haircut, new luggage even. Convention brochures promise a visit to swimming pools of top UK pop stars. Maybe, he hopes, Kylie's will be among them. She must live somewhere, England's a small island right? So far they haven't seen shit, just endless meetings and horrid breakfast food and finally a night out. And now a guy a bit older than he is apparently making some kind of pass down among their insteps, nudging his foot, which hurts anyhow with the incessant beat, over which Kylie's angelic voice keeps chirping, *"I'm burning up, I'm burning up. . . ."* Flattering if you weren't straight but he's straight. No really, despite the accusations flung at him by that bitch Charlotte of whom he'd once thought, finally a woman I can trust. *But Alan, if you've actually fantasized about men, you must really want them, deep down, face the facts Alan . . .* her voice, understanding initially, and him so grateful, so pathetically grateful he could open up, then her voice becoming a slash, a shriek *keeekeeekeeekeeekpittarumbapittarumba* Ever since that terrible night of confidences, the night of their breakup, he's only seen her in traffic. Let it stay that way. Over the years, he's rebuffed a few passes made to him by men encountered during business trips, on planes, or back in college days. He keeps these memories in a special place in his mind and trots them out when things get dull. His boss always sends Alan to visit with the gay customers, as a kind of bait, because he has the kind of body some men really dig, no sense being modest about it, but Alan acts oblivious, just treats the gay guys like he would every other customer. Polite, professional. Let's dig this hole! He has one memory of waking up in a hotel room somewhere in the West, a room not his own, his clothes torn, his body a bit bruised, his balls aching with an indefinable pain, and the bedclothes showing unmistakable signs of —what?—of something having happened to him. So maybe he did have sex, he thinks, but he doesn't know with whom or how. . . .

"Man up in the booth is having a party at his place," announces the foot guy, cupping Alan's ear. "Come to it, okay? It's quite nearby, we'll drive you. I'm Fitz," he continues, holding out a beefy hand. Alan looks him in the face and he's overtaken by a weird déjà vu, for the man beside him, once studied upclose, bears a strange resemblance to a singer from a long-gone pop band he'd followed in high school. All right, now a lot older, and chunky all around, red in the face, but still recognizable.

"I'm Alan," he says, then goes for it. "Are you Fitz from Making Waves?"

"Oh Christ," says Fitz, his face a big embarrassed grin. "They still remember!" He introduces Alan to his girlfriend, a tall, willowy, bored blonde. "But you're an American, how would you know of Making Waves?"

"Are you boys coming along?" intones Phoebe, her hand dangling a charm bracelet of car keys. "Or are we off on a stroll down Memory Lane to *Top of the Pops*?"

"Want to come up?" Fitz asks. "You see our DJ, our host—he's Chris from Making Waves. He was the cute one."

Alan is amazed. First free night in the UK and he's met a has-been popstar! "Can we stop back at my hotel for just a minute?" he begs. Phoebe shrugs, her eyes rolling. She's a stone fox, even a blind man could see that. Alan feels weak, all his expectations jostled and dumped topsy-turvy. "Hey Fitz, want a laugh? I thought you were a gay guy."

"He's not far from it if you ask me," Phoebe says. "And if you were to ask his wife she'd tell you the same."

"Women," Fitz sighs. "Can't live with 'em, or maybe not with just one of them." Out in the high street, the air so chill around their mouths, Phoebe and Fitz between them try to explain to their new American pal the strange vagaries of DJ Kris. "It's taken Chris a long time to distance himself from Making Waves," Phoebe says, generously. "He's not a boy any more, he's a man." "Spent years in the gym, he did, always looking for what he calls solid definition." "And credibility." So, Alan gathered, Chris's membership in Making Waves was a subject not to be alluded to. Fitz laughs and downs a tequila. "His credibility as a DJ will crumble into shit if people make the connection between DJ Kris and his cheesy pop past."

"Everyone knows, of course," yawns Phoebe. "He just acts as though, oh well, being a teen idol happened to somebody else."

"You must come to Chris's house," Fitz begs, "It's my birthday."

"Will Kylie Minogue be there?"

Fitz and Phoebe look at each other briefly, a European kind of look. "She's sure to bob up," Phoebe allows. "Durham is her home away from home and Fitz is one of her dearest amigos, aren't you, Fitz?" Alan feels his face swelling up into the shape of a plastic pumpkin, he's so excited and impressed. But he has to keep his cool.

Though confused and virginal, Alan has huge sex appetites. A compulsive masturbator, he likes to do it while driving, finds special thrill going by toll-taker during rush hour commute one hand on his dick. Almost caught several times. Has special g-spot excitement spot right under balls, narrow channel between balls and asshole, the perineum which he keeps shaved, lotioned, always smooth. He'd keep a dildo or vibrator or butt-plug at home, hidden in closet or somewhere, but he's afraid his house might burn down while he's at work and some fireman or other rescue worker would find sex device while he's absent. (No porn for the same reason.) So he's forced to resort to not so obvious household objects like cucumbers, et cetera. At the gym he's dangerously attracted, not to any man, but to their body parts, their funky clothes, few months ago he lifted a pair of boxer shorts instilled with a particular fragrance, sweat, piss, the whole drill. Bizarre.

He's decided he has the Christian Bale, *American Psycho* look. Now he wants the personality to go with it.

"You'll love the architecture at any rate," Phoebe says in the car on the way to Alan's hotel. "It's a Victorian building, once a police station, now converted to residential flats. When Chris bought the place it was nothing more than an empty shell, with cells. It took nearly a year of work before he could move in."

"Don't worry, Alan," Fitz snorts. "Chris took the cells out."

"And regretted that later," adds Phoebe. "Now tell me again why we're having to stop at the hotel?"

"So I can get changed," Alan says. "Won't take me a minute. And also I have some photos and I hope Fitz can sign them."

"You came here to England hoping to meet the pop stars?" Phoebe marvels, pulling in sharply under the hotel's beige marquee.

"I know," Alan says, hopping out. "How gay."

Up in the booth, enjoying the lordly height and the sweep of the floor, I just nod at Fitz, as if to say, *he'll do.* Pathetic that Fitz thinks he knows the kind of guy I like. Comical seeing this straight man cruise a club for tight asses; he's practically incapable of actually seeing a boy's ass. And all because in a moment of insanity I agreed to let him have his birthday bash at his place, seeing that Fitz's wife doesn't understand his need to scarf down cocaine, and his kids don't like him screwing other women, et cetera. You figure it out, I gave up long ago.

"You haven't told him about me," I caution.

"He knows nothing, nothing," Fitz says.

Fitz and I met long ago, in the 1980s, when we each answered an ad in the Sunday paper, "Make Top Money Now, Become a Pop Star," and attended auditions, mine in Hammersmith, him up in Glasgow. Behind the velvet curtain lurked pop impresario Simon Seymour, a devil in a polyester suit. Out of hundreds of applicants, he picked me and then Fitz. We didn't have to be able to sing or play any instruments, just had to, I don't know, "be." Whatever was in Simon Seymour's mind, which at that flicker of time was—"A new ABBA would really clean up." "And we'll call them 'Making Waves.'" I didn't actually meet Fitz until Making Waves shot its first video ("Sunshine Girl") in Aruba.

Two boys, two girls. The girls did most of the singing. I was the cute one, the one all the fans were supposed to fancy. Skinny and inoffensive. On the surface anyway. My hair naturally very dark and thick.

I can't even say the name of the band now without freezing up. I've changed my name, colored my hair, bleaching it blond for the last two years. I look nothing like the wide-eyed fuck puppy who used to dance around a stage, miming the words to terrible pop songs. A year after our debut we were dropped by the record company. A handful of minor hits, one flop album, and that was it. We were making waves no more, Simon Seymour told us flatly in his voice like an ice cube. Sometimes I'll see a programme on TV that asks, "Where Have the '80s Stars Gone?" and sometimes they mention Making Waves. Fitz appears on those broadcasts, but I've instructed him to tell them, "Chris? Went AWOL long ago, man. Haven't seen him since 1989."

Two queens have dug out my *Jaws* DVD and put it on. They're watching the scene where the shark attacks Richard Dreyfuss again and again. When the scene ends they skip right back to the start. The sound is turned off and a hard house track blasts from my stereo. I've no idea who these guys are. This is my fucking house and I hardly know any of the people here.

The mechanical shark is tearing its way into the cage. "Jaws should eat him," one queen says to the other. "Like in the book."

"Isn't the film better?"

"It's different. In the book Jaws eats Hooper."

"I wonder why they changed it."

"Don't know."

I do. They hired a team of experts to film footage of real sharks in the wild. During the filming one of the real great whites got caught up in the moorings of the empty cage and went into a frenzied attack. The producers were so impressed with this footage that they rewrote the script to incorporate it into the film. Richard Dreyfuss gets away before Jaws goes to town on the empty cage. I can't be bothered explaining this to the two strangers who are making themselves at home with my DVD collection. They're so fucked on E I doubt they'd understand anyway. They've grown tired of watching Dreyfuss wrestle the mechanical monster and are arguing about what to put on next. One of them wants to see the water-skier attack in *Jaws 2* while the other wants to watch the lap-dancing scene in *Showgirls*. I warn them to be careful with my discs and go to get another drink.

Over a dozen people sit round my dining room table, snorting and smoking. Colourful pills are passed around in neat plastic bags. No one cares a fuck about what they're taking. I lean over and take a line that's been chopped on top of a Shirley Bassey photo book. The girl whose coke it is smiles politely. If it wasn't my flat she'd tell me to fuck off. I don't know her name but I remember her from the club. She was dancing on a podium, bare to the waist; her pigeon tits hanging almost as far. Her skin is the colour of sour milk. This girl could really do with some sun. "Kris is here!" she cries. "Notorious DJ Kris."

The coke works fast. Tiny sparks of static electricity dance behind my nose. In no time at all it's tingling in my cock. My erection presses against my hip, inside my favourite white briefs. All my briefs are white. I have thirty-four pairs of the same style and colour. These are damp now. I'll change them when I get time. No one believes that a DJ sweats as much in his booth as all those dancers he is mixing into a frenzy.

Someone is playing with my CDs. They've exchanged hard house for disco. "Love To Love You Baby" is greeted with enthusiasm. The kitchen is full and the crowd spills out onto the fire escape. Fitz is doing tequila slammers off the washing machine. I slide over.

"Give me one of those."

He giggles, sloshing the gold liquid into a shot glass, slopping a good measure over the side. He moves the glass and licks up the spillage like milk.

"Having fun, Fitz?"

"Yes, cheers, Chris. Thanks for lending me the space."

His new girlfriend, can't think of her name, is slicing limes. The blonde bit. Her name's the same name as his wife, which is typical of Fitz and his distorted notions of loyalty. And handy in bed, he says, seeing as he only has to remember one name when he's shouting it out. She passes me a huge drum of salt and a wedge of lime. The tequila is the best, sliding down my throat like a squirt of my own come.

"You got some dykes fucking in your bathroom," Fitz says. He's finding it difficult to speak. "Had to piss in the garden."

"As long as they stay out of my bedroom." My bedroom is private. There's no need for anyone to go there. In the spare room there's a huge bed, equipped with all the toys, condoms, and lube that any of these freaks could want.

Fitz knocks back another shot and refills my glass.

"How many of these have you had?"

He shrugs. "Over thirty," he replies after a bit.

I knock back the second tequila but refuse a third, pouring a glass of Spanish red instead. I wander back through the flat, taking the bottle with me. In the living room *Showgirls* has won out. Elizabeth Berkley is thrusting her naked crotch in Kyle MacLachlan's face. He has a terrible hairstyle in this film.

There's an athletic-looking guy sitting on the floor beside the armchair, staring at the television screen. His legs are folded under him and he nurses an empty glass. I reckon he'll be a couple of years younger than I am, round about thirty. That's a bit older than my usual type but this fella is worth making an exception for. He has black hair, cut into a neat, boyish style and he's chewing his fingernails. He's wearing a tight black T-shirt and blue jeans, the body beneath is a result of work and dedication.

I pick my way through the outstretched legs and sit down beside him. "Hi," I say.

"Hi."

I detect an accent. He's American but I can't place the region. "You here alone?"

He looks at me and smiles. He's nervous. His eyes are as black as his hair. "I was at the club with a girl but I think I lost track of her somewhere."

"She could be outside," I suggest. "There's a lot of people in the garden."

"Actually she's not really a friend. I only met her this past week. She and I are on a course together. I don't know anyone in England so she invited me out with her tonight."

I'm already wondering what this guy's face will look like once it's stuffed with my cock. His name is Alan and he sells swimming pools. "I don't think there's much demand for home pools here in the UK," I joke.

His face remains stoic. "I'm here for a convention and meetings with your regional sales teams."

Now would be a good time to shove my dick in his mouth and stop him talking. Instead I offer him a drink.

"No thanks," he says, clinging to his empty glass. "And then in the club your—friend is he, Fitz?—invited me to this party."

"You have to try this," I say, pouring the wine. "It's good stuff."

I can tell he doesn't care for the taste but he drinks it anyway. "This apartment is awesome," he says.

Alan looks impressed. "Fitz was in a pop group, wasn't he?" For a moment I freeze. He can't have recognised *me*. I've changed so much. Besides we barely broke the band in Britain and Europe, we didn't get near the States.

I laugh. "Yes he was. Don't tell me you were a fan."

He laughs, looking at his feet. "No. I've never heard of them before tonight. I heard a couple of guys talking on the line to the bathroom. What were you called?"

"Making Waves."

"Must have been pretty cool. Being in a band."

"We were anything but cool."

"Tell me." He seems genuine.

"Rather not, if you don't mind."

"What happened?" Alan asks. "To the group? Why'd you split up? I'd love to hear some of your records."

"You won't be hearing them from me."

"Is Simon Seymour still alive?"

The two queens have skipped further into the film. They shriek loudly and applaud when Elizabeth Berkley shoves Gina Gershon down a flight of stairs. After a lot of clapping and hollering they move the scene straight back to the beginning.

When I turn to Alan I see that he's looking at me. He reacts like he's been caught and moves his eyes back to the television. He's finished his wine. I top it up for him again.

"This is a terrible movie."

"You say that like it's a bad thing." I love the way his nose wrinkles when he laughs. I imagine shooting my load all over his face, smearing it around his nose and lips with my cock, rubbing my juicy head against his closed eyelids.

He asks me if I have any pets . . . says he has to go to the bathroom. "I'm not used to drinking wine." He gets awkwardly to his feet and stumbles his way over to the stairs. He appears very self-conscious, as though aware that I'm watching him. I am watching him. His arse is a piece of perfection, so high and tight. I want to get my mouth in there and lick his crack until he pleads with me to put my cock in him. Until he gets on his hands and knees and shoves his arse at me, begging me to take it. I imagine he'll be a frisky and giving bottom.

Sitting on the floor makes my legs ache. I stand up and head back to the kitchen. It's cooler in here. More of the guests have moved down the fire escape to the garden that looks onto the river. Kylie Minogue is drinking a martini and eating a piece of pizza. She thanks me for the remix I recently completed for her. Fitz is still hammering back shots though they've run out of limes. It's almost five and things don't look like they're going to wind down anytime soon.

My cock feels wet against my hip. It's not sweat this time but pre-cum. I really need to get out of these pants and into a clean pair. I reckon it's about time I checked on things upstairs anyway. I take the bottle with me. I decide I'll look for Alan while I'm up there. I've got a gram of coke in my pocket and wonder if he wants to share it with me. Probably not. He doesn't even look like he drinks much, can't imagine him going for the party powder then.

Two clones are getting a blow job on the staircase from a third. I wink as I step around and warn then not to get come on my carpets. They all have very small cocks. Why is that? I've never met a clone with more than an average-size piece at best. It completely contradicts the tough, skinhead image. I'll take a well-hung chicken any time.

They are still queuing up to get in the bathroom.

There's a second bathroom in my bedroom but I don't tell anyone they can use it. It's strictly private.

My bedroom is the largest on this level. I chose it specifically for the size of the room and the massive window that looks out over the River Wear and the city beyond. You can see everything from there; the three towers of the cathedral, the castle, the peninsula. It's spectacular. But as I enter the room I'm confronted by an entirely different kind of view.

Alan is sitting on the corner of the bed. He's got his jeans around his ankles and a pair of my underpants over his face. The lid from my washing basket is lying on the floor along with a couple of dirty T-shirts that have been discarded in haste. He's sniffing my used pants.

A spit-lubed fist moves over a modest hard-on. A tight pair of balls hug the root and bounce against his hand with each tug. From my position in the doorway I can see that his scrotum and the passage beneath, leading to his arsehole, are exquisitely shaved. It reminds me of a boy, not yet developed. But his cock is definitely the organ of a man. It's not that big—I'm guessing just over six inches—but it's got a decent girth and a fat head.

He hasn't realised I'm here. He's too caught up in masturbating with my underwear. The anger I initially felt at the liberty he has taken has all but gone. But he's not going to get away with this intrusion. I'm going to have him. I step inside the room and close the door.

Alan bounds off the edge of the bed, dropping my pants. Panicked, he tries to stand up, reaching for his jeans. He stumbles and sprawls across the bed, face down, arse high. He still tries to pull up his jeans but they are caught around his meaty thighs.

"Stay down," I say. I'm over him, one foot rammed in middle of his back, forcing him into the carpet. He turns his head, wide eyes look frightened over his shoulder. The reverence in his face excites me. I apply more pressure. "What you doing in here?"

"I'm sorry," he stammers. His face is flushed, bright red around the brow and temples.

"This is my fucking room. It's private, you bastard." He tries to rise but I've got too much weight on top of him.

"I didn't know. Not until I was in."

"And thought you'd have a party of your own with my dirty laundry. What were you going to do, wipe your spunk up on my T-shirts and shove them back in the basket? Hope I won't notice?"

"I don't know. I didn't think. I couldn't stop myself." I'm looking at his arse which is just as ripe and perfect as I had imagined it. He has a nest of downy hair in the hollow of his spine that trails into the crack. I'm surprised he hasn't shaved this, considering how clean and smooth his balls are. His cheeks are meaty and round. I want to take a bite. Yeah, quite possibly I will.

I reach down for the pants he's been sniffing and take a hit on them myself. They're funky smelling, stained with yellow smears of sweat and piss. It looks like I've worn them for a gig. He couldn't have found a more unsavoury pair if he tried.

I grab his hair, releasing my foot from his back, and haul him onto his knees. He looks frightened. I shove his face against my crotch, letting him feel what I've got there. He tries to pull away but he can't. "Breathe in deep," I tell him. "Get it right from the source." My dick twitches and I know he can feel that.

I push him away. There's a wild, frightened look in his eyes. He's flat on his arse and his prick is jutting up towards his round navel. He doesn't try to get away. Now I know where we stand. I unfasten my jeans and ease my big cock out. His eyes widen. They always do. "Suck me," I tell him.

His mouth moves but it's a second or two before any sound comes out. "I can't . . . I never . . ."

I smack his face with my cock. The expression of shock is priceless. His mouth is hanging open so I grab the back his head and shove my dick inside. Surprise is on my side and I get to the back of his throat before he tenses up. Good, oh damned good. He hasn't got a clue how to move his lips or tongue around such a big piece but that doesn't matter. His warm, moist opening is all I need. I grip his head and shove deeper into the socket of his throat. His face is scarlet now and his cheeks are wet. I'm not sure if it's sweat or tears.

I move back a little, getting a rhythm going. I can tell how hard he's concentrating. I wonder how much experience he's had with men.

I'm big but most boys get used to me after a while. I fuck his face anyway. He hasn't tried to bite my cock off so he must be enjoying it in some way. I know I am.

But there's only so much cocksucking I can stand. It gets boring after a while. He gasps as I withdraw, open-mouthed and panting. His eyes are wordlessly asking "What next?"

"Let me see your arse," I say.

Alan hesitates, just for a moment, before turning round and lifting his arse for inspection. He pulls his T-shirt up to his shoulders exposing a broad, flawless back. I notice for the first time a small mole on his back, just above his right cheek. My eyes move lower, into the crack, towards his asshole. It resembles the mole in many ways, the colour is almost identical, only it's much bigger. Its colour reminds me of dark honey. I tell him to spread his cheeks a little and he does, stretching the opening. I can see something of the pink interior.

"Where's the girl?" I grunt. "The one you brought to the club."

"There was no girl," he moans. "I lied."

I get down and bury my face in his arse. His whole body jerks when my tongue caresses his hole. I'm certain this is a first for him, he's acting like a virgin. It occurs to me that he might have a wife and family back in the States. Maybe he considers himself to be straight. He wouldn't be the first straight man to drop his pants in my bedroom.

My tongue squirms around his hot opening. His has got a rich, manly taste. His arsehole quivers around my lips.

"Oh my God," he groans, his voice full of wonder. I'm pretty sure now that he's new to this. It seems strange, most men with any kind of interest in dick would have at least experienced something by his age. I fucked my first man when I was fourteen. He was a student, in his early twenties. He dropped his pants in the underbrush down by the river and let me poke him against a tree. I remember barely getting two thrusts in before I squirted a load in his arse. I was scared afterwards that he would expect me to return the favour but he settled for a wank instead.

And Simon Seymour, sitting with him on his Holly-wood poolside, him asking if I wanted to be a star, pointing at his tiny dick inside obscenely tight Speedos, me nodding, and then a half-hour later, me choking in the perfect blue water, head in shallow end, my arse up in the air with Simon Seymour sticking something in me bigger than that tiny little piece of meat, me choking, sputtering, from way above I hear, "That's the, huff, price of stardom, puff." Can still hear it in my ears today.

I've come a long way since then and I intend taking more than a couple of strokes at Alan's arse. He is on his knees, shoving his butt in my face, knowing what is coming. I feel between his legs, stroking the smooth path between his balls and his hole. That really gets him going so I back off, not wanting him to shoot before I'm inside. His bud is well soaked with spit so I stick a finger into him. He takes it easily enough. Nothing to worry about.

I think about offering him a line of coke but figure he'll panic. "Get on the bed," I say instead. "Face down."

He kicks off his shoes and wriggles out of jeans, climbs onto the bed in his socks and T-shirt. He lies on his front, spreading his legs. The guy's a natural.

I put on a condom and a handful of lube—then I fuck him. I climb on his back and slide my cock inside him, slowly to begin with. His body tenses with the introduction of my big head. I put my cheek against the back of his neck, pushing his face into the pillows. I tell him to relax, it'll soon get better. His arsehole is hungry; I know it can take me.

I fuck him hard and passionately, grunting with each stroke. His fists grip the pillows. My thighs slap loudly against the back of his legs. I love the squash of his buttocks against my pelvis when I drive it deep. In and out, in and out, I fuck him thoroughly, feeling his arse with every inch of my dick. I dig my knees into the bed, getting more leverage, holding his arse in my hands so he can't get away. Harder. The bed springs are screaming.

My orgasm is a long time coming. For ages it seems I am almost there. I keep going, harder, faster. I throw my full weight on top of him, my hips hammering. When it finally comes I roar with relief, squirting gallons of spunk inside him.

I pull out straight away. My cock, his buttocks, the back of his thighs are streaked with blood. Shit. He must have been a virgin after all. He raises himself slowly, testing his body. He's come onto the covers.

"Use the bathroom in there," I say. "There are towels under the sink." Alan nods, climbing off the bed. His steps to the door are unsteady. I grab a handful of tissues to clean the mess off the bedclothes. I go to take the condom off my still hard dick. Something isn't right. I wipe up some of the blood with a tissue and look again.

The rubber has split right down the middle. There's no semen in the ragged tip. Must have happened inside him. Fuck. He's left a folder on the carpet, plastic folder he must have dropped in his excitement over my laundry basket. Idly I open the folder, a clutch of 8x10 glossies slithers onto the floor. Kylie in a bedsheet, closing a blind from the *Light Years* era. Gareth Gates, his mouth a stuttery pout. And there I am, sliding out, my cheery mug from Making Waves, hideous yellowing headshot of young Chris, hair in tight curls, my autograph sprawling across it from a dozen years ago. No more. "For Alan, who must be my only fan in the USA, cheers, Chris from Making Waves 1987."

ZOO STORY

If you've ever seen *Cat People*, with Nastassja Kinski, you already know the first part of this story—how I became obsessed with big cats, the panthers and leopards at the zoo, how I battled my own best interests to become skilled in deceit. Mom and Dad had taught me right from wrong, but I dunno. . . . I was always a contrary boy. But if you've seen *Cat People* you know that I crept out of my apartment every night that spring, to drive to a distant neighborhood out by the beach. That I parked my car blocks away and jumped the fence—

—landing with a jolt that made my legs grow numb, to creep toward the cages, night after night, sitting there in the wet grass motionless each night, staring at the cats.

In the spring darkness they moved restlessly behind the bars, their great sleek torsos shifting like fluid in fur. The cages smelled like meat and urine, and something I didn't identify but with which I identified, a primeval scent, maybe blood or animal sperm? Tell me if you know. You know so much, having seen the film—what did you do, rent a video or something?

Anyhow in the dark I let my fantasies run wild. On the cold metal bars moonlight rained down, casting shadows across our bodies—mine and the panthers'. Wrapped in fur and sweat, they purred as they edged towards me, pausing to lick some salt out of a flat metal pan in the center of the cage. I wished the weather were warmer, I could have taken off my clothes—I felt such a powerful desire to do so, but no, it was pretty cool. At home I told my wife the grass stains on my pants were from touch football. That's an excuse I learned from watching TV detergent commercials. You always see these big macho hunks and from the waist down their tight, white, form-fitting chinos are long stains of grass and dirt rubbed in by hand, I suppose, by art directors of these TV projects. I wonder if the men are wearing the jeans while the dirt and grass get rubbed in and if they get sexually excited. That's the kind of thing I used to spend hours obsessing on.

I went to my family doctor, told him my desire to become a cat, he said he'd put me on Rogaine if my insurance would cover it. Or Prozac—or both. Otherwise he suggested that I do just what I've done—make countless trips to the Zoo, watch them in action, get my rocks off that way. Or buy a couple kittens from the SPCA, teach them to fellate me.

But one night I could stand it no longer. I rose awkwardly and took the few steps to the panthers' cage, and rubbed the front of my jeans up and around the cool bars.

It felt good, like the bursts of light and stars you see when Cinderella's fairy godmother taps her wand. My zipper was buckling up like a railroad accident—like some boxcar had collapsed, sending its freight careening down some gully. I guess nighttime is the right time? Like George Jones used to sing. Was it George Jones? Or George *Michael,* har de har har. Behind the bars a sleeping panther cocked open one large yellow eye. Growled softly. A rustling breeze bent back the nape of its black fur, and I pushed my groin closer to the iron bar, then edged my kneecaps in to produce some friction, a little. I wasn't going for any one thing: I just wanted to feel a little different. I thought back in a flash—in a series of flashes—to the way I look without my clothes; I felt proud of my body, its stark glamour in dark places. I remember thinking that if someone was watching me—say there were paparazzi around—my thighs and legs were in A-1 shape and my hair was lightly scented with shampoo. I had nothing to be ashamed of. I'm a man. A man without a conscience.

What made that night different from all the other nights of my life? Yeah, there was a full moon above: you could pick out every detail of the cage and the thick paws of the cats, paws that moved and shone like heavy beefsteaks, their tread a whistle in the dark. Yeah, a pool of slimy water spread across the concrete floor, and the moon was in it, flattened out and golden. Yeah, and there was this long turkey neck down my leg, hot and puffed up, and it was my prick. "Bill Barbour," I said to myself, "this is your night to howl." Maybe there's a little part in every guy that wouldn't mind getting clawed if approached in the right spirit. Or if hit up when he's feeling—down for other reasons. "Your night to howl," I repeated slowly, under my breath. And so saying I licked the cold bar of the cage and watched it steam before my eyes, before slightly crossed eyes, azure eyes the color of Icelandic seas and seamen.

But enough about me. When my mother was a girl, and pregnant nine months with me, a cat jumped into her lap and gave a ghastly howl, right at her face! Sent her into convulsions and labor. So I figure that's why I was there—it's not a sex compulsion, it's a gene or something. I wrapped my arms and legs around a tall cold iron bar and began to shimmy in, contracting and expanding the flexible muscles of my ribcage and hips, and feeling this icy heat at the base of my balls, flicker up bit by bit until my whole body was flooded with heat, a disaster for my suit—what a cleaning bill! But I felt for once alive in a primitive way, as I slithered between the bars to let myself be taken by the big cats. First they ripped off my jacket and pants as though they were so much cellophane. Then they stepped back as I swayed, trying to keep upright in my underwear, then they buffeted me with their snouts till I fell down among them, nude and helpless, a toy in the golden moonlight, my underwear a meal of shreds scattered like confetti around the cage perimeter. Next time you see kittens batting a catnip toy around, think of me on the cold concrete floor of the cage, pushed around, my neck snapping, their paws wet and warm on my chest, my legs, their claws retreating and contracting as they contrived to spread my thighs open to their hot rotten breaths.

* * * * * *

They cleared the cage and photographed my twisted torn body from all angles. Under luminol, the big cat's tongues and jowls glowed a ghostly green, and my wife fainted dead away, first fishing my cufflinks from the bed of flowers outside the cage. My butt was nothing but a leftover carved-up ham the day after Easter. My eyes, though, my eyes still in death must have been glittering, gleaming, pleasure-mad. Ask them to show you the autopsy pictures of—my eyes, my glazed demented eyeballs. When I felt the panther's slick meat inside me my blue eyes must have narrowed a bit, then rolled up into their sockets until only the whites remain visible, and I had to come, and I had to die.

SPURT

The blood jet / Is poetry.
—*Sylvia Plath*

My little car vibrated under me, as though its engine were announcing exciting plans to fall apart, but I didn't pay much attention. Tears were drying on my face. I was preoccupied, you might say; I simply hadn't the time for car trouble. For a week the temperature had stayed high above ninety degrees, and the radio announcers kept saying it was going to rain. Even at night the heat was thick and hot, like soup, but I kept driving, for when you're drunk, no challenge is quite beyond you. Traffic was light on the Long Island Expressway. Full moon, and moonlight revealing huge purple clouds scudding east, always before me, moving faster than I could. Squinting, I tried to read the hands of the dashboard clock. It was either 4:00 a.m. or 4:00 p.m. I was driving east, into the moonlight, away from the belt of lights that surround New York, and I was so drunk I could hardly keep my eyes open. My lids felt heavy, as though while I was crying some evil genie had implanted them with iron filings. My face felt like one of those cast-iron spigots that pour water into old-time zinc-lined, claw-footed bathtubs.

"I'm spent," I mumbled—that seemed dramatic. For luck I grabbed the bottle of Glenlivet that stood propped between my thighs, its long glass neck tapping the vibrating steering wheel. Single malt whiskey that had lain undisturbed in some Scottish cavern for more years than I'd been alive, and now, glug glug glug. Created just for me, on my dumb day of grief. On Monday morning I'd start cracking the books and really put my nose to the grindstone and work on the dissertation. You must keep going, I said to myself, like a coach giving a pep talk to a reluctant player. All the same, tonight, I would try to imagine that I wasn't returning to school—that I was done with writing and thinking—that I'd never met Tim Baillie.

Something magical about really flogging your car, and the clear stretch of highway ahead; and feeling the motor and its complex accoutrements shudder under your heavy foot. And dipping an elbow out into the hot summer night and watching towns go by like reflections in shop windows—whole towns and neighborhoods, gone, gone, gone. You lose touch with the world—a car is an island all its own, another world, a world from which, perhaps, you might never return. The radio, staticky and shrill, burst out with bass-heavy Motown, then the abrupt, insinuating guitars of the Eagles. A low-slung, dark car passed me on the right, gleaming like a streak of phosphorescence under a

Jamaican sea. Sucker must be doing a hundred easy. Lotus. Then the driver seemed to slack in speed and I was passing him. I saw his face—couldn't help it, he was staring right at me.

Cute guy, in a sleeveless T-shirt, blond, tanned, beach boy look, shock of curly blond hair on top of his head, big pink rubbery lips and dark eyes staring at me. Like he'd seen a ghost.

One hand rested on top of the wheel, lazily, as though he could drive without looking ahead. I sped up, and he sped up too. Cruise control. I caught him looking at me, again and again, and he flicked on the driver's seat light, a plastic dome that filled his car—for a brief moment—with a thin plastic light, like cheap statuary of the Church. I guess he knew how hot he was. His lips parted. I could see him trying to speak, or signal. Eighty miles an hour and his mouth was saying, "Wanna fuck?" I nodded, he nodded, I got hard, I shifted the bottle, the Eagles wailed, over and over, about how dangerous life was in California. What drips. Glug. Our cars kept passing each other, and the driver's image faded in and out of the open passenger seat window. "Let's," I heard him call, and my car leapt ahead a length or two. Then he was beside me again. A sheen of sweat made his upper body look wet, as though someone had pulled him out of the shower and thrown him into a moving car and said, "Drive!" He was my dumb guide racecar stud boy, come to lift the cover off this hot sultry night and show me love's underside. Or something.

I swung in behind the tail of the Lotus and we slowed down to a sedate 65 mph, into the right-hand lane, and a few interchanges later fishtailed out onto an exit, by a gas station and a diner. Under the purple neon lights of the diner we parked side-by-side. The Lotus was a gorgeous lime-green, a color that the purple neon and the purple clouds overhead kept remarking on, whispering among themselves. Buzzing about. Bzzzzzzz. "Where we going?" I asked—don't even know if I asked in words. When I jumped out of the car, the air smelled of burning rubber, and he was pulling off leather driving gloves. He was six feet tall, disheveled, with long ropy arms, supple with muscles and fading tattoos. Steam covered the parking lot to a level of about four feet high, up to our chests. The net result was I couldn't see if he was hard, but knew he was. A thick white steam like dry ice, or the hot air that pushes up Marilyn's skirt in *The Seven Year Itch*.

"I'm Scott," said my new boyfriend. "You know where the Meadowbrook is?" "The motel?" Calculations spun in my head like the apples and oranges in a slot machine. He shrugged, and the muscles in his shoulders rippled. He said to follow him. But first he kissed me, his big lips pressed flat against mine. When he broke away my mouth was aflame. "How old are you?" Scott said, like a challenge. I couldn't think if he wanted me older or younger so I told the truth. "Twenty-five." One time in life when truth seemed to do the trick. "Grand," he said, sliding into the Lotus butt-first. "It's room 813," he said. "We've got it all night." Foolish me! I thought "we" meant me and him; boy did I ever get that one wrong! I got back into the Maverick and took another slug of Glenlivet, then checked my wallet, then followed Scott down an access road past strip malls, gas stations, and into the huge, eerie, almost empty, motel lot. They should have called it "Salem's Lot." . . .

Spurt

Any of you ever been to the Meadowbrook Motel? I don't even know if it's still standing. In 1978 it was a sex motel, catering to the needs of suburban adulterers who could steal an hour from the PTA and the IRS and rent by the hour—what my cop pals called a hot-sheet pad. The Meadowbrook reared up its proud head like some Vegas monstrosity, huge lobby studded with Italian crystal and a marble fountain. On either side of this lobby two endless wings extended, big rooms joined by a kind of faux-balcony with wrought-iron railings. Privacy and discretion a must.

I couldn't see the Lotus, but I saw room 813. The door was ajar, and bright light edged the crack of the doorway. "Hello?" I mumbled, tapping, and slowly the door swung open. I stepped into a dazzle of whiteness and was grabbed from behind by a big burly guy: a thrill shot through my lungs like pure oxygen. "Hi," said a voice, teasingly. Big arms like bolsters against my chest. "What's *your* name?" His voice was dark and low, like some underground stream choked with weeds. When he ordered me to shut my eyes his words came out in a gargle. He twisted my wrists behind my back and held them there with one tight fist. I suppose I helped a little. "Where's Scott?" I said.

"Shot," said my captor.

"What?"

"I call him Shot," he replied, pinching my nipples through my white Brooks Brothers shirt. "I guess his name is Scott, but I call him Shot."

I relaxed a little and surveyed the room. "Why?" The salient feature of the Meadowbrook rooms was, and maybe still is, their walls—every available wall surface covered

47

with mirrors, like the end of *The Lady from Shanghai*. Mirrored ceiling, too, hung with the primitive track lighting of the '70s. Again and again my reflection gleamed back at me, and I could see the face of my captor. He shut the door with his bare foot, *slam*. Even the back of the door was a mirror. I guess there was a thermostat on one wall, but other than that there was only me, him, a TV, and a bed. Endlessly. And silent air conditioning—its thin metallic smell seemed to bounce back and forth between us. The TV was showing some closed channel sex film starring Marilyn Chambers. Marilyn was laughing her fool head off while jerking off one white guy and one black guy. The sound was turned down so I couldn't catch the dialogue.

"Because he's, like, well . . . he's shot," said the man behind me. "Didn't you see his eyes?" I'm thinking, God, I'm supposed to have sex with *this* guy? He was about fifty-five and must have weighed 300 pounds, wrapped in an oversized white terrycloth bathrobe, its sash underfoot on the red rug. "What is he, your scout?" "Ha ha ha," he laughed, as though I were joking. His unruly beard and jolly grin would mark him today as a Daddy type, a big bear, but back then we didn't have that type; to me he was just fat. But I was drunk enough to not really care. Weakly I held up the bottle of Glenlivet, waved it around. "Want a drink?"

"Shot's into bondage," said Bear Guy, making a face. "But not me, I'm only into eating beautiful ass; how about you?"

"Whatever," I said. The ruined king-size bed looked good to me. On TV Marilyn's face beamed, dripping with cum on her temples, eyes, lips. Okay, the linen wasn't exactly pristine—a thin strip of blood streaked the top sheet. "First I just want a drink."

Suddenly solicitous, Bear Guy led me to the bed and vanished into the bathroom. "Don't run off now!" I sat on one edge of the bed, taking off my shoes and socks. Soon he reappeared with a glass of ice. Glug glug glug. He said his name was Schuyler but all his "friends" called him Sky. "You've been crying," he said. I wondered if he was some kind of counselor in regular life. His big kind brown eyes. "Yes," I said, as I helped him insert his big hand through the zipper of my pants. "I've just been to a wake."

Sky squeezed my balls in that tender way some big guys have. "Ah, one of those long drunken Irish wakes. You look Irish."

"Yes," I said. I could see my face in the mirror, and beyond that I could see my own back. Everywhere I looked I saw me, sipping this motel glass full of that wonderful Scotch. Sophisticated. My cock was hard. I saw it. I saw it in the mirrors. It was everywhere, sluicing up and down through his hand. "This'll make you feel better," said Sky. He grabbed some change from the nightstand and put a couple of quarters into the frame of the waterbed. Instantly the bed started sliding and shaking up and down, to and fro, like an ocean liner on stormy seas. "Whoa," I said. "Relax," said Sky. Obedient, I shut my eyes and rolled onto my stomach. I didn't want see his belly, tons of flab folding over and reconstituting themselves as he bent to work. I lay slumped amid the big coverlets and stained sheets, hid my hot face in a pink satin pillow, ruffled with black lace. "Good night," I said sadly. I didn't want to puke. Sky tugged my pants down to my ankles, then peeled off my

tight white underwear, oohing and aahing like a connois-
seur, touching and nibbling. The bed kept shaking as he
parted the cheeks and licked the crack. At his muffled re-
quest—"Mmmftlmm?"—I raised my hips. I imagined my
legs sprawled, my bony ankles dull under the weight of
his knees, his bearded face buried inside my butt, a buffet.
Comfortable. His tongue darted in and out, in time with
the whirring vibrations of the waterbed, licking the walls of
my asshole. Nothing could surprise me, so when I became
aware there was another boy in the bed near me, already
passed out, snoring, I wasn't shocked, only pleased. I held
onto his waist, pressing my cock along his long thigh. Hispanic guy with nubbly little pubic hair surrounding this
enormous flaccid organ. His body was warm, he was naked, zzzzzz. An hour later, when I came to, he was gone.
I've always wondered who he was and what became of
him. The bed was still. Sky's quarters had run out.

And Sky must have run out too. Inside my ass I felt a little
stretched, but not much. My mouth was parched. Five-
thirty a.m. Scott was sitting on the other end of the bed,
fully dressed, making a phone call, by the mirrored nightstand. "You're up," he said to me, scratching the bridge of
his nose. "Grand."

There was still about an inch of my drink left—*thank
God*. Scott had two grams of cocaine that he said were worth
a hundred dollars. "On me." This was his hint for me to
fish them out of his clothes. They were in the right-hand
pocket of his blue jeans. I slithered to his end of the bed,
while he talked on the phone, I think to his girlfriend or
wife. I patted him down to find them, to find the tiny lump

the vials made in those slick blue pants. The inside of his pocket felt warm, greasy, like sticking a hand into a Joseph Beuys sculpture of fat. I looked over his shoulder and saw our two faces. I could barely make mine out; it looked like the mirror was melting it, like rain on spring snow. But his face glistened, tan and sweaty, brilliantly smiling. His eyes were blue, like mine, but darker, almost black. I pulled the stash out of his pocket and dropped the vials, lightly, on the big sloppy bed. He hung up and then we scarfed the coke. What the hell. After we kissed some more he jumped to his feet to remove the belt from the loops of his jeans. "You work in a garage or something?" I think I said. "Your clothes are dirty, man." Even his boxer shorts had grease stains, as though he worked on motors in his underwear, then wiped his hands on them.

Ever been really drunk, in a room full of mirrors? Liquor, brown and warm, slops down the side of your mouth. You can't swallow fast enough. Your kisses get sloppy, your vision too. All of a sudden there's a little click in your head, and the first person turns into the second person. That's you—Kevin. Have another drink. Don't mind if I do. You stroke the warm cock in your hand, you can't decide if it's yours or another's. Click. The second person slips into the third. Kevin rose suddenly, the chenille bedspread sticking to his butt, and made his way unsteadily toward the far end of the room, where a picture in a neo-Rosenquist style hung on the wall of mirrors. He thought it was marvelous.

Fine scars striped Scott's chest and back—thin shiny veins, like long gleaming tapeworms—and across both cheeks of his butt a thicker scar, of rough skin, as though he had backed into a hot pipe. Inside his head Kevin was, like, ????, but he kept grinning as though it was nothing out of the ordinary to see a guy whose outsides looked like insides. "So, you're into bondage?" Now it was Scott's turn to make a face. "Who told you that—Sky?" "Oh no," Kevin said sarcastically, "Lana Turner told me."

He wore Kevin's hands around his waist like a belt, but Kevin took them off and lit a Parliament, backwards, non-chalantly lighting its "recessed filter" so that acrid smoke filled the air of the mirrored room. Scott walked nude to the bathroom and flipped on the light. Blinking, he tipped a plastic glass sideways in his holder, one limp arm pointing at it, his fingers working, weakly, as though he wanted to grab it. "I'll take a drink too, you got any to spare." Like any other alcoholic, Kevin measured what was left in the bottle and tried to figure out if, indeed, there was any to "spare." Scott was naked in the threshold of the bathroom, and Kevin kept ogling him blearily. His body had the ex-traordinary angles of the junkie, the bumps and bones, the big thick red cock like a wind-up handle for the toy it set to motion. "Turn around," Kevin said. Scott complied. Kevin peered at his ass. It was big and full, a whole novel's worth. I could eat breakfast off that butt, thought Kevin, scar and all. He saw Scott's elbow working, moving like a piston from behind. Like, he's jerking off, kind of. When he turned again he had a hard-on bigger than a mackerel, and Kevin had seen a lot of fish. "Want another drink?" he said, pointing to the bottle that stood on the bedside. The alcohol sweat from Kevin's body gave him a chill on this hot humid night, just before dawn, and he shivered as though—*as though*, he thought, *a goose was walking over my grave.*

Brrrrr.

"Let's take a shower," Scott said. "I'm filthy." He told Kevin he liked being tied up to the shower pole—is it called a "pole?" Whatever it is that holds up a shower curtain—whatever it is that he was tapping like a woodpecker, in a rare burst of excitement. "Nah," Scott said flatly. "It's called, the rod!"—a word he seemed to find excitement in, as did Kevin: a phallic word, concealed yet radiant, like Poe's purloined letter, among the bathroom's pedestrian fittings. Then Scott further wanted Kevin to take the knife he held out, and slice him with it. "After that it can be *your* party." Trouble was there wasn't any rope in their mirrored motel room. On all four walls, on the ceiling, their faces, multiplied to infinity, represented an infinity of puzzlement, thousands of eyes darting around drunkenly to look for rope. Finally Scott gave up, shrugged, "No rope, let's improv." Improv? Very Second City, that boy! Very Lee Strasberg! For a few minutes Scott pretended he was tied, but that got tired. He stood facing away from Kevin, wrists crossed above his head clinging to the pole as though lashed on. He kept looking back over his shoulder, trying to panic. Trying to feel trapped.

"Hey," whined Scott. "I really could, you know, use some rope. And I'd like to do this before Sky comes back, if you don't mind."

There was a second click in Kevin's head—a click of clarity. He saw clearly, vividly, where he could find some rope—in the trunk of his Maverick. Viewed the mental image in 3-D. It was like getting sober. The third-person vanished. The second-person lasted only long enough for you to whip one of the motel towels around your waist and prop open the door with your pants. Then you were out in the parking lot, and pop! I opened the trunk, staring down at the rope Tim Baillie had hung himself with.

A tiny wind whistled under the thin cloth of the towel, tickling my balls. I bent over and took the extra rope. The leftover rope. Tim Baillie was dead now; I had just come back from his wake. He was my advisor in grad school, and I had slept with him to pass my orals. Do they still call them "orals"? I guess I used him, without many qualms: just did it, set him in my sights and knocked him down like a bowling pin with charm, Irish whiskey, and my big basket in the front row of Victorian Studies. "Kevin," he said, "you could have been a real scholar if you had anything in your mind." And now Tim Baillie—"*Dr.* Baillie, if you please!"—was dead.

Coiled loosely on the floor of the trunk, among pieces of an oily jack, the rope looked harmless enough. But just looking at it made me jittery, as though it concealed cobras. I remember fantasizing about an inquest where I would have to get up on the stand and some Perry Mason type would be snidely asking me, "Didn't you know he would use that rope to hang himself?" "No! No! I've gone through this a thousand times! Dr. Baillie said he wanted to pack a trunk!" "A trunk to death?" "No, no, an ordinary trunk!" "Mr. Killian, may I remind you that you swore to tell the whole truth and nothing but the truth?" What could I say? I knew I didn't love him, but wasn't giving him all that head enough for Tim Baillie? He had been closeted for forty years or more; I thought I was bringing a little sunshine into his elderly life. I remembered lying in his bed in his awful condo in Rocky Point with all his books on Alfred, Lord Tennyson stacked sideways on the bookcase, as though he didn't care enough about them to stand them up straight. I remembered listening with him to Willie Nelson's doleful *Stardust* album again and again—his favorite album, whereas mine was either *Radio Ethiopia* or *Sexual Healing.* Maybe I should have loved him. But nobody respected him, why should I? He was just this flabby fool with spots on his face that might have been freckles. He left a note, they told me: "I can't stand this heat." I didn't know, when he asked me to get him some rope at Smithtown Hardware, what he'd use it for. I remember his pursed lips when I showed him all the rope I'd bought, saying to me, "I only need about 12 feet, it's just for a trunk; I'm not Christo wrapping the Eiffel Tower." He cut off what he needed with a pair of cooking shears. Least he paid me for the whole 100 feet. Always this sarcasm, always the mockery, the checkbook, the despair. I thought *I* drank a lot till I met him—his eyes were the color of grappa, all the way through, no white, just this sick luscious purple-tinge color. Gulp.

When I heard about Tim Baillie's suicide, I was sitting at a table in a bar in Port Jefferson, reading a book, and nursing a bottle of beer and a glass of rum and Tab. The bottle kept leaving wet rings in the pages of the book. You know how Seurat worked? Placing millions of tiny dots of color into pointillistic masterpieces? I began to think, well, maybe you could do this with the wet rings of a beer bottle, and later Chuck Close took my insight and became way famous doing so. Oh Tim! If I made you feel second best,

Tim, I am sorry I was blind. Maybe I didn't hold you, all those lonely lonely times. Little things I should have said and done, I just never took the time, et cetera!

Room 813, Scott was lying on the bed whacking off, keeping his dick hard and his heels cool. "Grand," he said when I showed him the rope, and mimicked lassoing him. Expertly he tied himself up, lashing his wrists to the shower rod and needing my help only for the last knots. The rod was L-shaped, to match the contours of the bathtub below; its two ends screwed into two different mirrored walls, and a sassy full-length shower curtain of hot pink vinyl hung from it dramatically, the drag queen of all shower curtains. I stood behind Scott, kissing and biting his neck and shoulders, my hard-on poking between his thighs, his big butt. I gripped the knife in one hand, my knuckles white around its heft. He was on tiptoes, arms braced tautly against the frail metal rod. I flipped a hand between the part in the pink vinyl curtain, and turned on the shower, a rush of cool water beating on the other side of us. "You know what you're doing?" he said sharply. "I'm not a piece of meat, I just want to let some blood out. You don't hack me like you're at some butcher's shop." I saw him full length in the mirror facing us, on the other side of the tub. The hair under his armpits was blond, darker than the thatch on his head. His nipples were brownish-red, spaced far apart on his magnificent chest. "Right under my ribs," he said, "Let's start there." I could see how hard he was. His erection lifted his balls right along with it—everything pointed to the knife. I just wanted to fuck him but thought, well, later, later it'll be *my* party.

I took a deep breath and lifted the knife to his skin. First I heard a kind of screech, like two cats fighting. Then another screech, more protracted, from above my head. The shower rod screws sprang half out of their sockets in a noise of splitting glass and metal. My instinct was to jump back, anywhere, but there was nowhere to jump to. The knife fell from my fist. I tightened my hold round Scott's middle, his skin a blur. Another screw flew out of its seating and the shower walls collapsed. "Uh-oh," whispered Scott, and we began to drop, he right on top of me, he getting the worst of it for sure. Splinters of glass shot through the air, then whole panes peeled from the steamy bathroom walls, sticky with glue, and loud with crackling and smashing. The room was imploding. With a sudden crack, the rod bent again, into three broken parts, and all the curtain rings fell to one end like poker chips clicking on a croupier's table. Scott's body, still knotted to the mangled metal rod, fell to the bathroom floor with a heavy thud, though I tried to cushion his fall. Hot pink vinyl fluttered and descended over our heads. Slumped to the floor, Scott's torso sprayed blood, pink mist erupting up the side of the bathtub, mist that grew red at its edges. His hands were still tethered, with the hemp now wet, swollen. I sat on the floor, afraid to move, for the glass was everywhere, on the rug, on the pink tiles, strewn across the tan of his naked body like sand. And also I was afraid of sitting on the knife I had let go.

Mirrors, with bright colors zigzagging across them, his dick seemed a thousand feet long, like a string of sausages in a Chuck Jones cartoon. I kept seeing him bleeding out the corner of my eye, the way you might think you're seeing something when you're really paranoid. Peripheral vision.

"Guy, you all right?" I said.

His eyelids pulled up to reveal blue irises swimming in twin seas of pink. His lashes were incredibly long and from overhead, the gaudy light of the motel's fluorescent tubes threw long shadows onto his picked-over cheekbones. One large shard of mirror stood, like Stonehenge, embedded directly into his stomach, about an inch above and to the left of his navel. Another shard toppled over on his right thigh, propelling a piece of pink flesh, that looked like dog food, across the rim of the bathtub. The blood was everywhere. I was covered with blood, spots, streaks, puddles. But somehow I hadn't been hurt. I ran back into the bedroom to grab a drink, also to fetch a pillow to stanch Scott's blood; I had the word *tourniquet* in my head.

"I'm all right," he gasped. "Wow, I just wanted a little cut, dude, you brought in the whole artillery, didn't you?" "FX," I said. "Now help me," he said. "Help me come now."

I sat back on my haunches and used one hand to stroke my cock. With the other I held his dick, which hardened and throbbed to a vivid red brightness—its natural pink intensified by desire. I studied it before I began to pump: it looked angry, swollen, as though stung by bees. Blood and pre-cum, greasy in my loose fist. The aroma of blood: stale, tangy, older than either of us. Scott stirred, smiling, moved his head across the wet shiny tile. Gently I placed the pink satin pillow between his head and the floor; its black lace ruffle grew instantly darker with blood and water. "This is like some Mario Bava film!" I thought, scared to death, but horny, too. Scott's dark blue eyes fixed on some point on the mirrored wall, from which another face gazed back at him, mine or his. His tongue protruded from his mouth, like a dog in summer lapping up water. "Cool," he said.

His tan flesh, which should have been lightly dusted in sand, his beach boy look, spoiled or accentuated in scars, and everything pricked with glass, like a St. Sebastian I felt so sorry for, yet couldn't help. All I could do was jerk him off. That's all he wanted from me. His tongue touched the tip of my dick as I labored over him. Lick. Rustle. Spurt.

Again. Spurt. Presently I straightened up, creaking from my knees, and tossed a towel into the bathtub, so I could stand in it without cutting my feet on the broken slices of mirror. Then I stepped over his body and into the shower, let cool water rinse the blood from my arms, hair, crotch, legs. Through a streaming veil I watched Scott sink into sleep, as blood continued to pool up in all the concave sites of his fading body. Was he sleeping? Unconscious? His blond hair matted red, brown, black; his smile gave no clue, his big lips slack, happy, purple and gray as the petals of a sterling silver rose. I nudged him with the Glenlivet. He didn't seem to want a drink, again I'm like—*?????* Then I dressed, found my keys, left the motel. I guess.

RICKY'S ROMANCE

It all began when Ricky
It all began when Ricky
It all began when

—he stepped into the deserted copy room and closed the door behind him, with the furtive look of the temp office worker, something to Xerox held close to his chest. The copy room was nondescript, a box of close air, a gray carpet littered with bright white scales and dots and slivers of paper. Stale recycled oxygen, and the whirring sound, like white noise, of the mighty copy machine in the corner, surrounded by cases of paper, some half-opened, surrounded like a fortress by battlements.

There was a picture hung on one wall of the copy room, in a modern frame, an old-fashioned architect's drawing of the office building way back when. "History," Ricky thought, with the part of his mind that wasn't entirely preoccupied with getting in and getting out unseen. But he liked the picture where it was because in the glass that covered it, anyone standing in front of the Xerox machine copying something illegal could use the glass as a sketchy mirror and instantly know if someone else entered the room by the door behind, which otherwise moved silently on its hinges, without a sound.

Clever boy had concealed his contraband within a file folder stuffed with ordinary and authorized office mail

orized office mail

orized office mail, and he saw himself in the glass of the frame, a furtive hunted outcast from society . . . a temp worker at 101 California Street in San Francisco, and the editor and publisher of *Faye's Way*, possibly the best fanzine dedicated to the world's #1 actress, Faye Dunaway. Without further ado, he pushed the large square button on the Kona 10000 to restart the huge behemoth. Automatically the machine gave off a low groan that made Ricky start, trembling again. He turned back once more and cracked open the door to check if anyone was still in the halls of Ricocom International. "Though it's seven o'clock and the janitor doesn't start till eight-thirty," he thought. Still, some workaholics were known to come back after dinner and start working all over again on Ricocom business, whatever it was. Ricky had been working in filing for ten months and still didn't have much idea of what Ricocom did. "Why should I? I don't get benefits," he thought, closing the door behind him and returning to the now-humming Kona 10000. He opened his folder and

opened his

opened his folder and

and took out the twenty pages of Faye-related material that would make up *Faye's Way* #23. The Kona had a
little bottleneck problem as Ricky knew from experience:
it would take all twenty pages and reproduce them front
to back, two-sided, or whatever he selected, but the first
page or so sometimes shook uncontrollably in the auto
feed holder before being yanked into the hidden rollers.
Sometimes this resulted in a certain crease or wrinkle in the
large glossy photos of Faye's newest facelift . . . unfair to a
great lady and a great star. Ricky wet his lips and touched
his finger to his tongue. "Nice machine," he prayed.

As if in response the Kona's humming modulated
into a gentle croon, as if to say, "Feed me," and Ricky felt
a warm glow of affection. The twenty pages of Faye news,
gossip, and commentary disappeared one by one into the
lower depths of the 10000 with a bewildering ease. "Good
boy," he said. . . .

Mr. Tippett was gone, had left at 4:30 without saying,
as he sometimes did, "I'll be back this evening." Thinking
about Mr. Tippett, his cold, Nazi-like sneer and pale face,
made Ricky catch his breath a little, in fear.

For Hell would pay if Mr. Tippett caught him here by
the Kona machine, this late at night, with Faye contraband.

Ricky had started publishing *Faye's Way* in 1990 when
he saw how little serious work was really being done on
Faye Dunaway—"except by her surgeons," he thought—
she was in danger of becoming a joke and a has-been. In
1994 he had figured out HTML and ASCII and turned
Faye's Way into a web e-zine, with spectacular results. He
was now up to almost 110 hits a month, and had a paying

subscriber base of forty-five. Better than most commercial sites! In certain circles he, Ricky Mullins, was almost famous himself; his status as a lowly temp worker almost erased. Recently he had been chosen to write a blurb for a forthcoming book on Faye Dunaway's greatest films! *Faye mourns the death of Marcello Mastroianni*

Marcello Mastroianni

Marcello Mastroianni. I look kind of like her myself, Ricky thought, tapping his fingers on Kona's cool polished gray plastic surface . . . watching his face . . . his wide forehead, his blond hair carefully waxed in front to produce a kind of kiss curl over his brow, his almond-shaped eyes, green, though in the shadowy glass he could see no green, only a really good-looking face, part man, part boy. . . . I could be her son if she had one . . . but all of Dunaway's mothering instincts had gone into her career and her incredible love life. . . . Ricky admired that, but where had it all gone wrong for Faye? The catastrophe of *Mommie Dearest*, or the glacial Norma Shearerisms of *Voyage of the Damned*? Which was the defining moment in the before and after life of Oscar-winning Faye Dunaway?

Ricky's stomach growled, trying to tell him he had missed out on dinner with two chums. But his work came first and all over the U.S., and in two cities in Europe, forty-five Dunaway devotees were checking their mailboxes daily . . . Another page slid into the long feral slit of the Kona. "Good boy," said Ricky, rubbing the cool face of the machine, down by his crotch, almost as if he were rubbing himself . . . and as if by magic—some really sick magic!—the machine groaned to a mumbling halt. "Oh, shit!" On the bank of illuminated panels, Ricky read a bewildering message: "Try Error 78-E." A skeletal neon map of Kona's innards lit up and showed him what was all too plain, that one of the pages of *Faye's Way* #23 had gotten stuck inside the machine.

Quickly, with sweat popping up uncontrollably under his arms and down the small of his back, Ricky ran again to the door, checked the halls, and then returned to the sullen copier and bent to his task. Two enormous plastic (or metal?) doors swung open at the press of his fingertips, and he crouched on his heels, trying to see the missing page, hoping it wasn't crumpled, or torn. Somewhere in his head he saw Mr. Tippett's acidulous face, his grinning sneer, heard him whisper: "So this is your idea of Ricocom business?"

Hesitantly he reached inside, into the maw of gaping gears and blackness. The light wasn't too good in here, its fluorescence a trace, shadows on his bare arms. "Shit, shit, shit," he mumbled. "I don't see the fucking thing. . . ." The indicator said that the obstruction was in area J, but area J was almost further into the machine than his arm could reach. He stumbled onto his knees and thrust his arm into the cold, dark hollow. He was all too conscious of the incomplete, collated piles of *Faye's Way* #23 he had left in the sorting bin—what if Tippett came in right now, his pale eyes would dart to the unfinished heaps at once. His fingertips grazed at something that might have been a piece of paper, but he needed more leverage. I'm not double-jointed, he thought grimly. But he slipped off one shoe and wedged his foot inside the lower right corner of the open metal (plastic?) door, and managed to insert most of his upper body into the mysterious blackness. He felt the heat of plastic roller plates press up against his chest, his belly:

big round drums. Again the fingertips of his grasping left hand touched a smoother surface, what might be page 17. . . . "Why didn't you just stop at 16 pages?" he asked himself, without mercy. But he knew the answer, for pages 17–20 contained the results of his worldwide poll on what film would have been most improved if Faye had starred in it, the winner by a hair *Gone*

  with the Wind
  Gone with the Wind
  Gone with the

Ricky's foot curled and pressed further into the machine, trying to help his right leg bend with the intractable plates and drums. And then, with a little start of panic he (Runners-up: *Dr. Zhivago, Star Wars*—Faye as Princess Leia, more queenly, more elegant, than that tawdry Carrie Fisher—*Hello Dolly, Taxi Driver*—which Faye almost had!) he realized his foot was stuck somehow—and that the machine had started up again, in some indefinable way, its dead silence no longer a silence but an almost inaudible murmur, the sound you hear when you raise a seashell to your ear—but how? "How, for Christ's sake, how?" He tried to withdraw his left hand: couldn't. Slowly—were his eyes growing used to the pitch dark—the darkness was lifting and a strange, pale-green glow began to emanate from the innards of the Kona 10000. His head, sideways between drawers and rollers, felt enormous, like the big head of Evelyn Mulwray's retard daughter in Chinatown: *Is she your daughter? Is she your sister? Your daughter? Your sister? Slap, slap, slap, slap.*

She's both! And from behind, he could see the door of the copy room opening a crack—

And he heard a voice; oh shit, it's Tippett, Ricky thought. Scrambling to come up with an explanation.

The door swung open and he heard a sigh. "Mr. Tippett," said the voice.

"No, it's Ricky," he started to say, then thought better of it.

"Hey, Mr. Tippett, you okay?"

Ricky hung there, in a humiliating posture, half-in, half-out, feeling a red flush beat through his body from his face down to his chest and legs. He couldn't speak, but he was able to move his left leg, flop it from side to side in a plea for help.

"It is me, Osbaldo, Mr. Tippett," said the concerned voice. "Osbaldo, the janitor."

The green glow intensified.

Cooler air followed Osbaldo closer into the copy room; he approached Ricky's lower half with deliberate slowness and care. "Who the fuck is Osbaldo?" he thought wildly. "Christ, if the janitor's here it must be fucking 8:30." Drops of silvery moisture, like mercury, appeared on the convex face of the drum an inch from his nose and mouth. Then he felt Osbaldo's hand on his waist.

"I have waited so long for you, Mr. Tippett," said Osbaldo.

Clunk, clunk, the janitor's mop and bucket fell to the floor as Osbaldo crouched beneath Ricky and, with eager hands, felt up and along his ribcage, under the strained cotton of his Polo shirt, and Ricky almost cried out.

And he was thinking, my God, I had Tippett all wrong all along!

Wondering how little he really know about people—

"For you have driven me half loco with my longing for you, and I, only a janitor for Ricocom, Mr. Tippett." The Kona 10000 began percolating, and squares of greenish light began to appear before Ricky's eyes, gathering density until they resembled some kind of holographic—panes—of stained glass, or blotter acid. . . . "And you have walked in front of me numerous times showing me your proud walk and your tight Nordic buns of steel, Mr. Tippett, and now you offer me your buns of steel, fucking *maricon.*"

Osbaldo, hesitant no longer, quickly took Ricky's thin belt out of the loops of his Dockers, and then took down the pants, sliding them down to his thighs, where the unfortunate angle of his trapped leg gave the janitor pause. He swore in Spanish and, from the pocket of his uniform, withdrew a razor blade. "You like to get fucked, Tippett?" Osbaldo cried, as he tore the cardboard cover off the blade. "You and your stuck-up ass too good for the common man."

Ricky felt the smooth imperceptible sound of his pants, deftly scissored in two. Osbaldo's big callused fingers grabbed the waistband of his Ron Chereskin boxers and, as quickly as you or I might open an egg, he had them sliced off; Ricky's ass was bare to the air. "I lick your ass as I do every day of your motherfucking life, Mr. Gary Tippett," moaned the janitor, applying his rough tongue to the distorted globes. Ricky felt himself grow hard as the janitor darted his tongue inside his exposed asshole; his erection poked uncomfortably along the gray plastic toner cartridge. The hairs on the backs of his legs rose and fell in response to Osbaldo's vigorous rim job. Between slurps, he emitted muttered words of affection and class hatred, mingled with renewed gobs of sticky saliva.

"You wiggle white ass once too often at Osbaldo, Mr. Tippett!" The hologram plates seemed to pass through Ricky's face without hurting him. His irises were huge in his head, swollen, like his vulnerable asshole. The noise all around him increased in volume and in vibration. "That's right, motherfucker, shake that booty. You like my tongue up your butt don't you, *maricón*?"

With implacable knowledge, the great drum inched forward, like a guillotine, and Ricky saw—or *felt!*—the pages of *Faye's Way* #23 begin to photograph *themselves*, a montage of Faye's face first tiny, the size of a postage stamp, then larger and larger, billboard size, only to disappear into darkness. Then, a moment later, the face again, tiny, big, huge, black. In each interval the blessed instant of darkness, then the dawn of green, as regular and monotonous as a heartbeat. Ricky hardly registered the shock when Osbaldo thrust his fingers into his gaping asshole, so intently was he watching the miracle of reproduction. From the ceiling of the machine a light gray powder began to descend. "I fuck you with janitor hand," Osbaldo announced, suiting the action to the word, and punctuating each thrust with a slap to Ricky's naked butt. Ricky was getting harder and harder, more excited, and his hard-on strained against the slowly rolling canister of toner. The slither of a zipper. The fingers disappeared and the head of Osbaldo's huge dick touched the wet ring of Ricky's anus. "I'm ready as a rooster, Mr. Tippett," sang the janitor. "You are gonna get the bonky-bonk of your motherfuckin' life, executive pig."

Osbaldo's legs and torso were stocky, heavily muscled, and rippled as he plowed Ricky Mullins from behind, his hands, reeking of man-ass, clutched the panel of the big Kona for support. His fingers pressed every button on the front panel as he felt his dick swell up inside the groaning asshole, for to fuck Mr. Tippett had been his dream ever since he came to this country and saw the haughty executive, bent over a desk examining figures. "One fine day," he had thought to himself, "those buns of Nordic steel will be mine to manhandle." And now he was fucking the man himself. The Kona 10000 leaped to life, issuing page after page of Faye Dunaway's tormented face . . . and then Ricky saw—

his own face—

page after page—after countless page, spitting from the machine—his face in ecstasy, speckled with toner—"I fuck you with Latin beat, like Selena, turn the beat around, *corazón*"—the huge dick filling his ass—his balls tight and swollen like green grapes—

everything green, then black, then the stark white of bond paper—

his balls banging his ass and Osbaldo's dick jumping in and out, the copier buttons like piano keys, like the piano keys David Helfgott plays in *Shine*—

Faye Dunaway, not Lynn Redgrave, as the woman he marries—

Rachmaninoff—

motherfucker—writhing and twitching—Completed copies of *Faye's Way* #23, stacking themselves neatly in the collator tray on the left; then the copies shoved, thump, thump to the floor, replaced by new uncalled-for copies . . . more paper outside than inside the machine—

"Fuck me," Ricky thought, "even if I'm not the guy

you think I am," and he began to shoot all over the inside of the copy machine . . . great helpless spurts of seed cum like white-out . . .

While Osbaldo's face bore the ecstatic stigmata of the possessed, and his hands dropped to his sides. "Even if I'm not Tippett," Ricky hollered, tho' neither of them could hear him speak and indeed, so great was the Kona's roar inside his ears, and so great his orgasm, that he was not sure he spoke aloud, or if the machine spoke for him.

When Ricky woke, next to the Kona machine, his body was glazed, just like an eclair or jelly-donut. His razored boxers and slacks were folded neatly to one side, atop the eleven hundred copies of *Faye's Way* #23.

All of them neatly stapled in the upper left hand corner, gathered into cardboard boxes, ready for UPS I guess.

All of them with his own picture on the cover, his tongue halfway out of his mouth, his eyes rolled back in his head like one dead.

On top of his chest a post-it note, "Sorry, *hermano*, wrong fuck," it read.

Nothing more.

DIETMAR LUTZ MON AMOUR

I've got to approach this sleeping story on tiptoe, sneaking up behind it while its snores punctuate the pillow.

When I met Dietmar Lutz, the heat of high summer scorched the back of my neck, and a flash rainstorm turned the dry leaves of Golden Gate Park into wet, green, flapping fish. I found shelter inside a museum, the De Young, and made my way to the basement, a basement with high windows set up against the roof, windows that let in a little greenish light and a fog of steam in San Francisco, the city where I live, the city where, without knowing it, I'd been not living but merely waiting, waiting for him for many years. The rainy walls of the basement, where I was lounging atop the broad surface of a metal cart on wheels. All of a sudden this guy is, like, "Hey, you're not supposed to sit there," and with a push he starts wheeling me down the hall on the cart. Pretty fast—I was clutching the sides of the cart and kicking my feet out onto the wall to slow him down. I had barely the chance to look at his face, but his uniform commanded my attention, the uniform froze me in terror—the primitive terror of authority that has plagued me ever since a difficult boyhood, when my father, a handsome Irishman who resembled the young Tyrone Power, was so good to me that he all but ruined me for other men. Love is like madness, and to write about love in this time of general madness I must adopt the uniform of my oppressor, the painter Dietmar Lutz, and I must approach our story carefully, while it lies sleeping, in the basement of a museum under heavy rain and about to be demolished. Soon the museum will become a ruin, and it is as a clinician and historian that I come upon the story, sleeping, its head a mass of blurry fevers and dreams, drooling on the white pillowcase, a silver feather of drool connecting its red lips to the white linen, then, boo!

He and it and history and my age all prompt me to tell this love story as though Marguerite Duras were watching me.

The story ravishes me; I admire it from afar.

"I'm here on business," I told the guard, summoning up the tremendous dignity you need to try to keep your butt on a moving cart. I didn't know his name. Perhaps his badge showed his name, but I couldn't read it. He was wheeling me down the cavernous halls at a speed faster than that at which I usually drive. Perhaps twenty miles per hour. I don't know what this is in kilometers or whatever they use in Germany, in Düsseldorf. He would know—but he's out of my life now. Can't ask Dietmar Lutz, even though

I know his name as well as I know his painting, his heroic painting of me and my wife, which stands above our toaster oven on top of a long line of Dodie's cookbooks, a site specific, a site he came to my apartment and picked out of the walls. I watch the painting, thinking it's moving. It's catching up to me. Like a cart out of control.

The De Young's deserted now, won't reopen for another four years, and in the meantime the building will be torn down and a new one built on this site by the preeminent Pritzker-winning architects Herzog and de Meuron. I didn't think anyone would mind if I came in, got out of the rain. Past a door that said, "Staff Only. Door Will Sound," I slipped, squish squish, down a long flight of marble stairs. The hallway space cavernous, twenty feet wide, twenty feet tall, stretched at least two hundred yards. A few wrapped packages—canvases?—stood tilted against one bare yellow wall. I had a book with me, thought I'd kill some time.

"Here on business," he repeated, slowing down a little. Color rose to his cheekbones. First thing I thought of was, *he is so much younger than I.* Funny how that's what you think once you turn 48, how half the world is younger and maybe one-tenth is older. He was about my height, and very slim, with fair skin and a face round as a peach, and his eyes, set behind his fair lashes like plums, were a deep mauve color like petunias. These distant eyes seemed kind, as though a kind nature battled for breath through that uniform of cold gray.

And then hearing him speak, his voice a hollowing echo in the humid chamber, and I'm, like, *he's German or something.* Dressed as a guard, he wore a thin cotton uniform of gray, like a jumpsuit, a black belt around his waist, with a roll of keys that would choke a monkey. On his breast a tiny pin read "Guard." He was steering me towards a corner of the hallway where I could hear a video playing. A tiny TV, set up on a milk crate, showed some videogame I had trouble identifying. I thought maybe I was under arrest for trespassing. I tumbled off the cart when he stopped rolling me. Found my feet, got my bearings. The videogame flickered and blurred—gladiators frozen, silver swords in air.

Piled up like logs, rolled-up carpets made a little fortress out of this corner. My guard checked his watch, then sat back on one rolled rug, his feet flat on the floor. "So what's the story?" he asked.

His bright purple eyes boning into me. It all clicked in that he was bored and looking for something to distract him. And that was how I met Dietmar Lutz—big steely flashlight on his hip, Sam Browne belt, and an earpiece plugged into his right ear like a wax seal. "I'm Dietmar," he said. "It's very good to meet you."

He unrolled a second rug, flipped it over, its nap was woody looking, the way rugs look underneath. He had painted over it in big wet strokes of titanium red and pink and white; this huge canvas looked like a face. I swear to God, it looked like the face was grinning, grinning at me, giving me a mental command, saying, "Fuck this guy." Not like, "Fuck him," but "Fuck him in a sex way." Tentatively I looked at Dietmar's mouth, I thought I could see a slice of red tongue peeking through his teeth—seductively? I raised my hand, trembling, till I touched him. His shirt seemed to glide an inch up his rib cage as I touched his side. So hot in that museum basement he was sweating, wide circles of black in the gray of his uniform—under his arms, down the small of his back. Otherwise he seemed cool, his mouth cool as a raspberry in some ice cream treat. "Business," he repeated. Gee, I didn't know then he would destroy me through the passion of living. It just seemed like, well, a half an hour thing then bye bye, back on 5 Fulton, and then home to my wife.

"Your favorite writer?" "Chris Isherwood."

"If you could bring one book to a desert island, it would be—?" "Aldous Huxley, *Island*."

"Your favorite artists?" "Hobbypop." "Least favorite artists?" "Hobbypop." Over the next few weeks I grew tired of hearing of "Hobbypop Museum," some kind of artists' collective in Düsseldorf and London, to which Dietmar belonged, to which his first loyalty lay. He was always planning some new "Hobbypop" project, vast installations in ever-vaster gallery spaces. Architects, sculptors, musicians, and painters formed a floating nucleus which could expand or contract as Dietmar decided. Whenever we were together, he would wriggle from my arms to check the "Hobbypop" website and see how many "hits" it had gotten since the last time he checked. Me, grasping the cuff of his pants as he wriggled away towards the glowing screen.

"Is there food you're allergic to?" "Not that I know," he said.

"What's your favorite food?"

"Gaisburger marsch," he said, stumping me. I rested my head on his chest, on his nipple where earlier the pin had been, his guard pin, still attached to his shirt. I know so little of Germany, oh, maybe more than some, but not knowing *Gaisburger marsch* underlined how far away I could ever be from understanding Dietmar Lutz. We were both artists, but what is art, this little nothing that doesn't count for shit. Think about what Eva Hesse wrote, "Art doesn't last, life doesn't last, what does it matter?" I wrote in to the Poetics List bragging about an interview Brian Pera had done of me; all the questions were, simply, the names of movies, directors, actors, and I responded sort of off the top of my head—but not really of course. And Brian Pera writes a little bit about my book *Argento Series* to introduce the article. What do you know, but this awful asshole from—New Zealand!—writes me privately and says, "I've no doubt that all this is fascinating but I hate Hollywood and movies and people who are involved with AIDS: I dont want to know anymore about the corruption of U.S. movies." He signs it "Richard" as though we're intimate. I'm so upset by this nasty who-asked-you type of attack, I can barely look Dietmar in the face. I'm feeling xenophobic—shaky with this haze of hate like, suddenly, I hate people from New Zealand—and—this spills off, of course, into my hating people from Germany, as my father did.

Dodie wrote to "Richard" as follows: "I saw what you wrote to Kevin, and this is so stupid and corrupt, I'm appalled. You're hating hearing about people involved in a plague. You should keep your right-wing opinions to yourself."

Unabashed, he wrote right back. "Dodie. Why should I: If I have right or wrong or left wing opinions they are mine: the American Constitution and probably the United Nations Charter etc guarantees the right of free speech. There's too much political correctness: I'm sick of bloody queers. Richard." Dodie and I stare at one another as though to confess to each other our equal ignorance of the United Nations Charter which is probably *so important* to those horrid *Kiwis of New Zealand*! In the meantime as I found out more about Dietmar Lutz, I wound up meeting many of his cohorts in the Hobbypop Museum, all young and frighteningly talented people, mostly from Germany but one from Britain and one from Russia, and I wound up writing a play in which they acted out the parts of German artists visiting San Francisco. I cast Dietmar as Anselm Kiefer, the heroic painter (b. 1945) of enormous, slapdash chiaroscuro history, mostly for the pleasure of seeing him, Dietmar, paint during each performance of our play a portrait of his colleague, Sophie von Hellerman, who was playing the supermodel Claudia Schiffer (b. 1970)—also from Düsseldorf, a train with no end. This was in the autumn of 2001. Only yesterday really. When love flattens out proportion, the body of the affected one becomes a sensitive membrane, a clock without hands.

Dietmar was super-clairvoyant. When he went out in the street, he would soak everything up until he was ready to faint. When he saw an ant crawl across a pavement, into a crack, he became that ant. When he came across a bloodied T-shirt in a North Beach dumpster, he followed the flux back through time and felt the blood flow. He saw me through time, back before I was married, to the early days of San Francisco when acid and disco and bathhouse sex were my whole life, and he saw or felt all I had forgotten or tried to. With two fingers he plucked my dick and examined it, its tiny imperfections, all the men it had been into, and the way it had run my life. All in all, I'm a healthy sort—he sensed no major calamity. He was right—about the dick thing. "It's no hazard," he said.

"Well, I'm no Forrest Tucker," I said, uncomfortable. I tried to cross my legs but he kept one hand under my balls.

"You are ashamed," he told me. "Your body is not what it used to be when you were young and when you were a drunk."

"I gave up drinking and then—and only then!—did everything give out." I grabbed his cock and held it in one hand, then the other, trying to "read" him as he had read me. But nothing. For all my imagination this cock told me only that it was erecting itself in this one moment, now, in my wet palm, my stubby wet fingers, one of them sporting a wedding ring at a crucial joint. Dietmar grunted as the gold of my ring touched the vein under the head of his penis, he moved forward, I smelled his scent as he pressed his head into my neck. "Who is Forrest Tucker?" he asked.

I could hardly explain it to him—I barely remembered Forrest Tucker myself, the affable, slow-burning actor from *F Troop*—until I recalled that Tucker had played Auntie Mame's Southern suitor in the Rosalind Russell movie. Then he seemed to recognize the name. "Not so pretty a man," Dietmar said.

"He's just a shorthand for a—He was famous in Hollywood for having the biggest cock in town."

"Which you don't have."

"Which I don't have."

"That's okay, my Forrest Tucker," he said. I felt all the heat in my body bolt into his hands, where he held my cock, divining its history. "You are a man and, like every man, you have your own secrets."

I pulled away his uniform from his shoulders, felt his skin through his white cotton T-shirt, felt a scar there, thick and veiny like Harry Potter's lightning bolt. Felt it through the material. My eyebrows raised. "I was attacked by a heavy metal fan," he explained. "Don't ask."

"Was he from New Zealand perhaps, that's the land where they hate the bloody queers."

"No," said Dietmar. "Not from New Zealand."

"I'm going to come in your hands," I confessed.

"Just wait a minute if you can, Mr. Tucker."

His pants fell down to his shoes—those sharply polished black shoes, like a dancer's. His bare legs, lightly dusted with blond hair, and what looked like large bite marks on both legs, from calf to ankle. He squeezed my cock and all its history splattered over his legs. I felt his very breath on my face. My history of pain and lying and longing now written on his skin. "You're very close to the general idea of what a man is," he told me, "an American, and that's what makes you unforgettable, that's why you make me cry, you are completely generic like all men here in America."

"Who bit your legs, Dietmar?"

"Pack of dogs."

"What music do you like?" "Electro . . . Kraftwerk . . . Mahler."

"Have you got any bad habits?" "Liar."

"Are you good with children?" "Yes."

"I would like to paint your picture," he offered.

"I'd like that."

"A painting of you, and your wife, a double portrait."

"She'd love it," I said. My mind spinning through various combinations. "When we're old, we could sell it and live." Rossellini's *Germany Year Zero*, the boy Edmund jumping from the ruined building to his death, a splatter on the street. Nothing there in Germany. Nothing but death and the human spirit crushed. Neo-realismo. De Sica, *Umberto D*, except with me and Dodie as two distinguished intellectual professor types evicted, trying to find good homes for our cats Blanche and Stanley but scaring off the little children we hope will adopt them.

Quizzically Dietmar picked up a brush. "As you please, but I want to visit your apartment and pick out the space on your wall where it will hang—until you sell it."

His brushes were so thick and long you could hardly imagine painting with them—painting a house, maybe. Where was the delicacy? I didn't want any rough stuff—only in sex. Not on the wall.

"How old were you, when you had your first sex experience?"

"17." "Are you top or bottom or both?"

"Both." "Have you been tattooed?"

"No." "Why not?"
"Boring."

"I had a funny feeling when I met you, Dietmar. I flashed back thirty years ago when I was a young boy, working in a shitty summer job in a grocery store." He nodded. "On Long Island, which is a suburban attachment to New York."

"Where De Kooning lived, and Jackson Pollock," he said. "I have been to Long Island."

"But further west, halfway between Manhattan and the Hamptons. In this horrid little town called Brentwood and I"—I could not continue, the memories too painful, the memories of Brentwood. The difficulty of speaking, of thinking, about a time when I was mad. Just as in love this illusion exists, this illusion of being able never to forget, so I was under the illusion that I would never forget Brentwood. Just as in love.

"Have you loved many women?"

"My sister Maureen," I said. "And when I met Dodie Bellamy I fell in love as one might fall in love with a man." I counted for other women. "Two."

"Many married men in California, even in San Francisco, the soi-disant 'gay capital.' And you—obviously you are gay?"

He lay on his stomach as if asleep, his eyes turned toward the wall. The rolls of carpet, covered with black rubber. His back was bare, his legs as well, the vivid bites of the foreign dogs climbing up his calves. I lowered my hand, palm down, and slid my fingers under the neat waist of his jockey shorts, felt the rubbed surface of the dimple above his buttocks. His legs crossed, then uncrossed, as though I had made him move through the action of my hand, its gentle pressure on his skin. I knelt beside his body and licked at the frayed cotton that enclosed his ass, my mouth a factory of saliva, my tongue wriggling across the curve, and then like a dog I bit him, but not hard, not hard enough to break the skin, the cotton parted with my teeth. One finger moved under the elastic pouch and into the warmth of his asshole, felt the heat there, the warmth of his secret place. "Are you from a large family?" I asked him, my tongue in his crack, my nose snagged in his underwear. "Yes," he told me. "Four brothers, one sister, about fifty cousins." I put the sister to one side and concentrated on rimming not only Dietmar Lutz, but a whole slew of German brothers, all at once, perhaps all bent over some kind of horse trough in the middle of a war-torn Middle Ages landscape. The brothers clenched each other's hands almost like lovers, their eyes snapped shut as though under lock. Some cousins in the background throwing horseshoes. Maybe the sister up in a turret room writing in her diary about the strange American visitor and his penchant for Dietmar, his romantic friend.

That same night, Mark Bingham overslept—partying too late the night before at his friend's thirtieth birthday—and missed his plane back to San Francisco. No problem, he'd catch the next one. New York's skyline looked bleary, wobbly, from the fourteenth-floor window, floor to ceiling, of Billy's apartment. Mark stepped into the shower and washed all the sleep out of his eyes, doing a set of kneebends in the tiny stall to save time. Trapped on a plane for five hours, on the endless flight from Newark to SFO, he'd often found a good workout beforehand helped his muscles relax.

"Bye, doll," Matt said at Newark Airport, his motor running. Mark grabbed his two little bags and headed for the Starbucks. Kept telling himself to cut down on coffee, bad for his wind, but first thing in the morning he needed it, and the plane was supposedly full, so he wouldn't be stretching out. At the counter he cocked back his head and downed a handful of white pills—melatonin—leopard's bane, daisy, clubmoss—the homeopathic route. And whoosh, no more jet lag. Doctor in the city had told him once what everything did but Mark had forgotten. And "clubmoss,"—what a name! Reminded him of clubfoot. He looked down at his own feet in the trim black trainers. Wadded up the Starbucks cup and sailed off to security. He had his John Grisham book, and a pocketful of those tiny disposable camera photos of Billy's party to remember all the cute guys whose numbers they'd scrawled on the back. His thin little white laptop fit right under his arm like a cricket bat.

"Flight 93, nonstop to San Francisco, proceed to gate 48." You could listen to those announcements forever and still not hear them. Even the children nearby seemed already to have learned to tune them all out. One little girl wore a pair of headphones almost as big as she was, white, feathery, with Big Bird's head on top. Her mouth was slightly open and she was humming some insipid Mandy Moore number about *I'm too young to have any problems.* Her father, Mark noticed, was wearing a pair of baggy LL Bean-style Boy Scout shorts; slouched as he was in the uncomfortable modernist waiting-room chair, you could see almost right to the top of his inner thigh. Alas, there was nothing there! It's like he has it tucked up into his butt like some tranny. The man looked up from his guidebook and met Mark's gaze, blinked. Mark nodded with his eyebrows, held his—his what?

Mark had met Matt online; they often joked about that. In the "Husky 'n' Stocky" chatroom on AOL, and Mark had registered under the nick "BigNDumbNY." Now he was thinking of spending his life with him. Funny the way things turn out. The buzz and hum of the airport glided above his head. In his pocket his cell was buzzing but it was probably Amanda or someone from the office, in other words, later, dude.

"What was it like, the member of the man who destroyed you?"

I tell him it was like an object from the beginning of the world, coarse and ugly, petrified in a state of desire, always full and hard, painful as a wound.

We weren't always locked in a puzzle in the basement of the Museum. Like any other European on a visa, Dietmar wanted to see the sights. We went to see Tony Bennett at the Plush Room on Sutter, that old boîte cabaret feel. and Tony Bennett pouring his old lungs out. "And maybe, Kevin, you can tell me, where is the house of Anton LaVey? I took the 1 California bus out so far, but couldn't find it."

"You didn't go far enough," I said. "It's out there, but way out."

"I'm planning a film on his house; are visitors allowed in?"

"It's all boarded up," I said.

"Kenneth Anger filmed *Scorpio Rising* there."

No, he did not, you know-it-all. I thought these words but did not let them pass into speech. Kept them instead inside my head with a cloud of buzzing flies. Dietmar went on to elaborate about the hidden history of San Francisco and how all our most sacred and evocative sites are oc-cluded from view.

He sketched out the lives of Aleister Crowley and Victor Neuberg and how the two men, given over to Satan through the study of ancient ritual, had gone to the desert and committed a single act of sodomy under the Moroccan moonlight, and how Crowley had turned Neuberg into a camel through superior magicianship. It was a story that had long been the basis for many of my most romantic fan-tasies. *Know-it-all, how did you know?*

Whether or not Anton LaVey was a real Satanic mas-ter or merely an amusing American charlatan like Colonel Tom Parker or Orson Welles didn't matter to my German friend. He was determined to see the house and make a film there. I decided to take him in my '86 Dodge Aries station wagon, a winsome baby blue in color, seemingly the oldest car still extant on the streets of our beautiful city. His camera was small and neat as a lunchbox. He kept it on his lap, purring, like a cat or vibrator, his eyes alert as we passed avenue after avenue through the ugli-est part of San Francisco. This was a man with more fo-cus than I needed. "Jayne Mansfield and Sammy Davis Jr. were among the celebrity converts of Anton LaVey," he told me. "The big white woman and the little black man, both musical."

"Except for Jayne Mansfield," I agreed.

"It is said Anton LaVey died during a manifestation of the Evil One in his sleep. That day the skies were dark with flying snakes above Geary Street. LaVey was a chum of 'Wild Bill' Donovan of the OSS, the predecessor of the CIA, and Donovan gave him copies of the secret Satanic papers of Adolf Hitler after the relief of Berlin."

"Did you meet Glen Helfand here?"

Dietmar frowned.

"He's an art writer," I offered, "and he's in our play."

"Oh, yes, very pleasant."

"Glen used to work in this bookstore out in Stonestown—a mall nearby, horribly tacky and suburban—and Anton LaVey was his customer. His client?" I couldn't think of the right word, the word bland enough, for a European to understand me. "His patron?"

"What was he like?"

"Just what I asked him! All Glen could remember was that he wore makeup on top of his head. I'm, like, 'Makeup?' And Glen is, like, 'Yeah, like—foundation. To give him that all-around youthful look.' And of course I asked Glen what books—if any—did LaVey buy at the mall?"

Dietmar laughed at me. "You are a novelist, the man with the questions. Always the questions about human behavior and tastes."

I didn't reply. Low engine noise rumbled from underneath the wagon, under our feet, rattling the whole front seat. Nothing out of the ordinary. A flock of Korean schoolchildren in matching pink puffy jackets was crossing the street, attended by an elderly black woman in a suit. I was the novelist, consumed with questions and hungry for answers, but they didn't have to be the true answers. I wanted Glen to say, *Jude the Obscure*, or *Valley of the Dolls*, indeed any title would have done. Instead he gave me that blank look, smiled, then threw his hands up, and said, "I was young, I don't remember, how did I know from Anton LaVey? I don't know—maybe, *Interview with the Vampire*?

"You know what Anton LaVey bought from Glen?" I said to Dietmar Lutz, shifting into drive as the light turned green. *"Interview with a Vampire."*

I watched his pale delicate skin crawl with a frisson, half glee, half horror; his face grew pink with sensation. "For real!" he cried.

I realized I could go on lying to Dietmar Lutz—*or were they lies? They were kind of the truth!*—and enchant him for a while, by identifying his pleasure centers and manipulating them across the chasm of cultural difference that made us one man here driving, the other man over there, filming our approach to the Black House of Anton LaVey. Thus love gives savor to the lie, injects flavor into the apple's core. Whenever I saw an apple fall from a bag, I thought of Dietmar Lutz, his big thick brushes, his inquisitive eye, his dick pointing at my mouth or nose.

"Ever been visited by the dead?" "No."

"Do you follow football?" "Not any more."

"Worst job you ever had?" He considered. "Night shift in a hotel."

"What's your favorite musical composition?" "'Neon Lights' by Kraftwerk."

Finally we pulled up in front of one of those ticky-tacky houses out in the Sunset, checked the address. California Street, between 23rd and 24th Avenues. In front of us rose the Satanic house, but what an aesthetic let-down. For one thing, it's now a total fixer-upper. Dilapidated, grim, horrid. Plywood squares cover its windows, except for the broken triangles of dirty glass right under its eaves. You picture a lot of pigeons nesting in there up in its attic. There's no lawn to speak of, the whole thing might have been painted black at one time but now the black is streaky. When he saw there was no entry, and not much to film, Dietmar hit on the idea of folding paper airplanes and trying to sail one or two through the open dormer triangle. "We'll write messages to the dead Anton LaVey, on the paper planes."

We sat on the hood of the station wagon, ripping out sheets of paper from Dietmar's "San Francisco Trip" notebook he'd bought in the Haight—wild Austin Powers psychedelic colors all aswirl, a groovy souvenir. I used a black Magic Marker to write, "Hey Anton."

"I love your country, they sell the 'Black Magic' pens!"

"No, they're just called 'Magic Markers,' this one happens to be black in ink." I couldn't help it; I just started talking like him. Black in ink indeed. For when I was with him, nearby him, my blood slowed down to a coma level, and my brain would speed up trying to anticipate him. Dietmar put the cap of his Montblanc in his shirt pocket and wrote, "Dear Anton LaVey, make yourself manifest among us for my video camera." Three more times I wrote, "Hi Anton." We folded our papers and zipped them into the open air. Over and over again, these little paper planes, that kept bouncing off the walls or conversely, would perform this kind of loop-the-loop air-show maneuver and seemed to go everywhere else but the window we aimed at. "Total bust, homey!" Meanwhile the camera recorded each of our attempts and who knows, over in London, Dietmar Lutz might be editing this footage into something real right now. I loved him. You might think him deep in the same overwhelming absence. Only his breathing was left sometimes. He acted as though I were sleeping. Sometimes you might think that everything that was happening was a lie between two countries. I bent him over a desk, spread his butt in front of me, and fucked him for the good of world peace. "Does he exert a malevolent influence over your work?" he asked, his jaw a blur. I looked at him in disbelief. "Who? Anton LaVey? I have the supreme pleasure of telling you I have never even heard of him!"—these violent thrusts up his ass while I denied the occult powers of his Master. He clutched the far legs of the desk, his knuckles white, taking me in, taking in my denial as well as my acceptance.

"Have you ever been hospitalized?" "No."

"Do you practice any superstitions?" "Successfully voodoo once."

"What weather do you like?" "All."

We had our arguments, many of them about the allegedly low qualities of American newspapers. Like one who cannot help probing a sore tooth with his tongue, Dietmar abhorred the *San Francisco Chronicle* and yet read it feverishly every day, fascinatedly turning page after page and parsing every print ad. "It is not even a newspaper," he said. "There's no attempt at analysis, no foreign news. It is— what do you call the paper you wipe your ass with?"

"Toilet paper," I said thinly. "Why? Because there's nothing in the news about Düsseldorf?"

"About anywhere in Germany!" he sputtered.

As though Germany was the center of the world. He held up the offending sheet. There was a nice color photo of our local anchorwoman who was in dutch with local police for throwing eggs and tomatoes at some tree surgeons who were operating chainsaws beneath the windows of her penthouse apartment in Russian Hill. "Tsk-Tsk, Terilyn," read the headline.

"I suppose you wouldn't be happy unless the front page covered the 20th anniversary of Romy Schneider's death."

"No, but nothing about Germany at all? It is not to be believed!" He stood and began to mimic wiping his ass with the *Chronicle*. Then he dropped the paper and rolled some paint on his big wide brush, a creamy mauve. I watched the paint drip from the brush into the open pan. It made a satisfying sound. "And what is all this fuss about Mark Bingham? You people in San Francisco seem to believe he was some kind of hero!"

"Of course he was a hero," I said. "He was the hero of Flight 93, as you very well know. Don't be perverse just for its own sake."

"How do you know he was a hero? Look, I'm sorry the plane went down and all, but—"

"He and several other brave Americans wrested the

plane away from the terrorists. It crashed, okay? But at least we thwarted the terrorists' plans. And Mark Bingham we like in particular because he was from San Francisco. He was our homeboy, you might say. His office was just around the corner from my apartment, on Lafayette."

"And he was gay," Dietmar shouted, "and so all the gay people have their hero in this city. And yet the truth is, nobody knows what went on in that plane."

"The FBI played the tapes for the families."

"What does that prove? You've got all these business-people on cell phones calling their wives and saying, 'Arab men have taken over the first class cabin, we're thinking of retaliating.' I repeat, my friend, you have blown up Mark Bingham as you might blow up a big balloon for your gay parade."

"But all his friends say he was just the type of per-son who *would* take charge. Hey, before he came along, gay rugby was a laughingstock and he made it happen single-handedly. He was the sparkplug of the San Fran-cisco Fog."

Slap, slap, the brush dripping with mauve oil tra-versed the shapeless canvas. I saw a tiny mauve trickle slither down Dietmar's right hand towards his wrist. For a moment he said nothing, while I berated myself once again for using the word "sparkplug" to a foreign boy who couldn't be expected to understand me. It seemed a kind of cultural imperialism. I kept replying to myself, "But he's the tourist, not you. He's the one in an outside country."

"Can you see into the future?" "No."

"What has been your longest journey?" "Three months all over southeast Europe and Egypt and Israel."

"How much do you spend on clothes per year?" "Little." "How much would you like to spend?" "A lot."

"And now tell me about Brentwood," Dietmar commanded. His breath rose up from his lips into my face. I saw two red bars, like silk stripes, rise from his pale face across his cheekbones, as though he felt exerted, or was blushing. "Brentwood, the town where your shame occurred."

I played dumb. "Brentwood?"

"You are no Forrest Tucker, my friend Kevin. You cannot act to save your life. Brentwood," he reiterated. "Halfway between Manhattan and the Hamptons you said. You told me it was there, in that town, that your trauma took place, when you were a boy in your teens. What happened? Let the talking cure begin, let's waste no more time, tell all to Dr. Lutz."

"Oh, you are an analyst too, as well as a painter!"

"That may well be," he replied. "You wouldn't know, but it isn't easy managing an artists' collective for as long as Hobbypop Museum has stayed together. Some say this is to my credit as a—" He fumbled for the word. The bars of red on his face glowed softly under the dingy basement light.

"Peacemaker?"

"I was about to say, as an artist. But today, we must all seek the spirit of understanding as well as bow the knee to our Muses."

I clapped my hand over his mouth, beseeched him to refrain from asking me about Brentwood. And yet, bidden now, the spirit of that horrid town rose writhing above our bodies, in embrace, writhing in clouds of billowing smoke and suggestion. "Picture an American supermarket, in the little town of Brentwood, a mile or so from the famous girls' school that was the real-life model for the school Hayley Mills attended in *The Trouble with Angels*. A supermarket, rows of food products and butchers in the back, along the front glass windows a line of cash registers manned by idiots, waiting on idiots. They bring their carts of food to the cashiers, and lay them out for inspection; they pay for them there. This is where I worked, when I was seventeen. Checkout boy, they called me. In Brentwood, where anyone could come to the plate glass window of the store and stick their face to the glass and watch me."

I would never forget it. I'd be busy counting up the food stamps proffered to me by my customers, and I'd look up at the outside, at nature, at the parking lot, my attention diverted by movement, and there I'd see a little gang of high school boys and girls framed there, directly behind me, watching me as though I were a clown in the Cirque de Soleil. I couldn't hear what they were hooting and hollering. Soon as they had my eye, they'd leap into an array of movements, flapping impossibly limp wrists, smacking huge kisses at me, grinding their groins against the window. One girl took out a looseleaf notebook and held a few scrawled words against the glass, "DIE FAGGOT."

Other employees of the grocery seemed to notice, and yet not to notice, this daily disruption, which always occurred around the same time, maybe 3:30, when I figured the godforsaken last bell of Brentwood High must have rung. One worker, Gina, would roll her eyes in mute sympathy. Customers would ask me if the boys and girls out there on the sidewalk were my friends.

To some I replied, "Oh yeah, pay them no mind, they're just goofing on me."

To others I couldn't speak, for the tears were building up behind my eyes and filling my throat. Constantly afraid, part of me was paralyzed, like the proverbial deer caught in the headlights.

"Did you never confront those boys and girls?" asked Dietmar.

"I was too damn scared," said I. "Petrified. I couldn't even give them the finger. When I left the store at night I was terrified they'd come find me and beat the shit out of me before I could get to my car."

"They were probably gay themselves," he said, to console me perhaps.

"Ah, I had read enough watered-down Freud to think of that one myself, but, no, I don't think so. Douglas Crimp says that gay people often excuse the homophobia of others by giving them the benefit of overdetermination. For often enough we have fallen in to group instinct ourselves, often enough we have joined in with the straight majority and helped them bash other gay men and women. By this same token, we often suspect the oppressor of being secretly gay but, he says, this is only rarely the case. And my manager would come over, say I was causing a ruckus, ordering me to get those kids to leave."

"Did any of them ever come into the store?"

"No. . . . Yes, one time one did, this big boy I had named, in the back of my mind, Leo, because my mother had a pet dachshund called 'Leo,' and this boy reminded me of that dog. Leo was in line, my line, I looked up and he threw down a package of Fritos on my belt, my moving conveyor belt I kept going with the hydraulic squeeze of my foot on a floor pump. There was Leo, asking me, would I give him a blow job."

"And this was your trauma?" he chided. "Tsk, tsk, Terilyn."

"No," I said. "That was just something that happens to everyone in America. My trauma was—"

"Let's do this later," said Dietmar. "Hobbypop is having a big show at Anthony d'Offay and I must plan." He saw my blank look. "The famous dealer in London! The one they call, 'Prince of Darkness.'" Prince of Darkness! My mind was making two twos all over a giant blackboard that reached out in all directions to cover the world, and its stern face fairly bubbled with my sums: 2 + 2, 2 + 2, 2 +2, and oh baby, so many fours! "I will be returning to Düsseldorf to marshal our London invasion, but first," he said, "you and your wife must pose for me. I want my portrait of you to hang over your refrigerator at home, in your sunny kitchen on the top floor on that building South of Market."

"Dietmar, I forgot to ask you—oh, so many questions before you go, before you leave me forever."

"You knew I never planned to stay in San Francisco, that my home is far away."

"I knew."

He thrust an arm into his jacket. "Always with the questions! Very well, ask away, with you I have always been truthful at any rate. Far more truthful than you have been with me."

"What time period would you like to have lived through?" I asked. I watched him dress for our cold autumn evening. "Or is the present the best time for you?"

"'What period'? Any—maybe time of my birth—1968."

"Where were you when Berlin Wall came down?"

"Düsseldorf."

"When Princess Diana died?"

"Berlin." There are probably other remarkable events by which even a man like Dietmar Lutz could mark his momentary staying on this earth, the way it is said that at a certain time every single person on this earth knew where they were, what they were doing, when JFK was shot. But I couldn't think of any, except the destruction of the World Trade Center—except the day Mark Bingham was killed. And that was still a sore subject between my painter friend and me. September 11.

September 11, 2001. "Have you ever seen anyone die?"

"Once at a car accident."

"First movie you remember seeing?" *"Winnetou 1."*

"What languages can you speak?" "Latin. English. French. German."

"If you were a jewel, which one would it be?" *"Bergkristall."*

Later, at home, I asked Dodie, "Kins, do we still have a subscription to Netflix?"

"We just started it," she reminded me. Her arm filled with brown paper bags from Rainbow, she was just edging through the door. Blanche and Stanley came out from under the bed, wondering if she'd brought them any treats. "But if you think it's too expensive we can cancel it."

I took one of the bags from her, we humped them

through the little hallway into the kitchen. Clunk, without even watching you could hear one of the books fall onto the floor. "No, I like Netflix; do you think they have *Winnetou 1*?"

"They have 11,000 movies," she said. "What's *Winnetou 1*?"

"Let's rent it," I said.

"Is it German?" she asked.

"How did you know?"

"Gee," she replied, sarcastically. "How did I know?"

"*Winnetou 1—Apache Gold,* Old Shatterhand and Winnetou, the chief of the Apaches, confront murdering gold raiders in Apache territory. Old Shatterhand's a German writer who can kill a man with one blow of his fist and who yet prefers mercy to murder. And there's Iltsche, Winnetou's faithful steed."

"Sounds like a pip."

"What's this book on the floor?" I asked rhetorically, on my knees in the dust. "Oh look, it's Marguerite Duras."

"You're my little St. Anthony," she observed. "I've been looking for that book for my class."

"Dodie?"

"Mmmmm?" She swung open the refrigerator door, surveyed its shelves. "I didn't get soymilk, damn it."

"What's a *bergkristall*? It's like a jewel I think."

The door slammed shut. "I don't know," she said. The pages of Duras riffled in the breeze as she blew dust from its edges. "You know who might know is . . ."

"Dietmar's leaving," I said. "But first we have to pose for our portrait. When are you free?"

"This is a busy time for me," said Dodie. She put down

the Duras novel and picked up her little black appointment book. "When does he want to do it?"

"Anytime. . . . Soon."

"Have you ever been hypnotized?" "Never worked."

"Do you know many jokes?" "Always forget jokes."

"Do you believe in the afterlife?" "Yes." "Have you seen any ghosts?" "Once the soul of a dog."

"You are good for me, you are killing me."

Mark couldn't help but notice how many big guys had boarded Flight 93. At six-three he himself was no slouch and his body, boisterously muscled, perfected after years of rugby and gym work, always felt constricted in airplanes. His bare knees rubbing up against the serving tray of the seat ahead. Even in first class, and he felt sorry for the poor cattle jerks who couldn't afford but to sit in cabin. Yah, he was large, but his fellow passengers dwarfed him—big, hefty guys and he found his attention wandering from the inane United commercial about fastening your seat belts. He wondered why they bothered showing these warning movies before every flight; surely no one was watching it at all. Not a head was looking up. Oh yes, there were one or two. Arabs by the looks of them, intent, as though they had never seen a video before, one with a little beard that looked itchy. The Gershwin "Rhapsody in Blue" theme spread its tinkly, expansive piano kitsch throughout the compartment, and Mark wondered which of these men were headed, as he was, back to San Francisco, and which were going on to L.A. You could kind of tell by their outfits. Money changes everything.

Then there was time to sink into a deepening spiral of worry, an atavistic twang like an arrow, worry about his finances and how to stem the apparently unstoppable dot-com crash that was slicing his business to bits. Who was rushing, now, to hire Bingham Associates to promote their new electronic gateways, when all gateways were permanently jammed or disappearing? Down to one client, it was sometimes days before the phone rang at the office. He'd let the boy go who fetched him coffee from Ted's Market. It was all him nowadays, chipper, putting on a brave front. You always found ways to make yourself busy—more than busy, almost unavailable. At night he looked at his face in the mirror and practiced that big Tom Cruise smile. "They call me 'Bear Trap,'" he'd say to himself, in the twilight, his teeth in the mirror glinting an impeccable grin. "So bear up, boy!" The fellow next to him kept talking on his cell, a series of gruff calls, each ending with "Let's roll," then he'd snap the phone shut and replace it in his lapel pocket for a minute, then seemed to think of another client, and fished it out again, flicking it open with a kind of gay wave of his wrist. Probably never gave a thought as to how he looked. People with a lot of customers never do, Mark thought sadly. They've got business to transact. Maybe he'd have a bloody mary or something, or would Business Flip Roll Guy think badly of him for drinking so early? Todd Beamer. "Hair of the dog," Mark practiced rehearsing, as though talking to an understanding bartender, like Brick at the Eagle or Jimmy at Lone Star. Maybe he'd ask Todd, if that was his name, if he'd like a drink too, kind of break the ice, find out more about that wedding band. Was it Ramadan? Was that why all the Arab guys seemed so tense? He raised his hand and depressed the green square.

But no steward appeared. Suddenly Mark was very aware of how quiet everything was. And Todd's talking at him about the World Trade Center—*the what?* Partly he was thinking, those damn stewards, who seem so cruisy when they greet you on the way in, all disappear to the back and rank the talent. And partly he was taking in Todd's white, drained face, *the World what? World Trade what?*

"Quick," I said to Dietmar. "Name six colors without even thinking."

His eyes slid closed and through his lids I saw the colors appear to him like the hours on a clock. "Red, blue, yellow, pink, green, black." He named them with no punctuation, red blue yellow pink green black. Then he opened his eyes and hid his grin behind his hands. "I knew you would ask. All my lovers ask me to name the colors. Don't know why. They know I'm a painter is my guess."

"The German Fairfield Porter."

"Once I'm naked I guess I look like colors spout out of me like—" He shook his fist in a familiar masturbation gesture, but to Dietmar it seemed to indicate: champagne. "All men ask me, not just you from America. And now what do you think of Fairfield Porter?" We were quoting from a recent review Dietmar had read of his work, some London show, in *Flash Art*, that had dubbed him the Fairfield Porter of Düsseldorf. "The thinned-down acrylic that Lutz works with rapidly soaks into the canvas, leaving a clean fabric surface stained by the pigment. The loose but energetic brushstrokes are expressed in the differentiation of color density rather than in any surface texture, giving these paintings a squeaky-clean quality. Diminutive knots of paint, however, appear here and there to redeem these paintings to establish the physicality, if not the muscularity, that we have come to expect from this expressive, gestural style of painting. No nervous impressionist or aggressive expressionist brushstrokes here though, these works are resonant with cool." I laid my body heavy over his, sacks of groceries on a moving conveyor belt, and stared into his face. Perhaps I was drawn to him because his work is so much like that of our beloved Southampton painter of pink porches and washed out beachfront, sad burghers slim in apache tops. Except "out" of course. And German. And fifty years younger. "I tried to get away from Long Island but you can't take Long Island out of the boy."

"Red, blue, yellow, pink, green, black." Somewhere in there were the colors of our flags mixed together like the long-ago incantations of Aleister Crowley. Somewhere a red and blue wagon filled with cyclamen, yellow and pink, pulled by a little black boy in an oversized green Roc-a-Wear tracksuit. The boy plods on under the hot Long Island sun past Fairfield Porter's shingled house. "You make what we've got together into a love thing," Dietmar chided me. "And really it is no more than two cultures wanking each other because the world, right now, is a frightening planet."

"I was arrested," I told him, rolling over. "That was my trauma, my arrest at the store."

"In Brentwood."

"Not far from Fairfield Porter's house."

"What did you do?"

"Stole money from the grocery store," I said. "Every dollar bill I took had been earned by me, or so I thought, my fear had earned me recompense, but legally it was theirs, those wretched store people."

"Some kind of scam? How did it work?"

"At this date I don't really remember. But say a customer came in with a cart full of groceries and a handful of coupons. I'd take the coupons, one by one, add them up, then subtract them from the total. Five dollars worth of coupons? I'll take it off from the top. Ring up a smaller amount. At the end of the day I'd be fifty, a hundred dollars richer." I felt that my body on his body recapitulated the scene of my crime. My terror when pulled off the line and taken to a black office up a rickety flight of stairs. How I wanted to fling myself off the stairs like the boy, Edmund, in Rossellini's film, *Germany Year Zero.* They told me I was a thief, a liar, that no one would ever trust me again, no one would ever hire me again. My future in retail was over. At the end I was reduced to saying, "Thank you." I was thinking in my head of the teens on the far side of the plate glass window and how I would never have to see them again, jeering at me, threatening me. "Thank you, thank you." I was all crying and my nose was stuffed thick with snot.

"Did you ever see *Germany Year Zero*?"

"No," he said. "Heard of it."

"See it," I said. "When you go back to Düsseldorf or London, and you're thinking of the painting you did of me and Dodie, see this movie, *Germany Year Zero,* and I'll be there, on the screen." Then I said no more, for my mouth was thick with his cock, which swelled up against the roof of my mouth, as one who might blow up a big balloon and pull it down Main Street for the gay parade. His little balls, their wiry hair thick and scratchy underneath my bottom lip like I was wearing one of those "soul patch" goatees like "Tony" used to wear on 24 until he shaved it off and lost his looks, and suddenly my throat was shot full of fluid. If I could take his essence, I thought, it was only something that was endlessly proliferating within Dietmar Lutz. "When you're frightened do you move or breathe more quickly or slowly?"

"Slowly."

I took his cock from out of my mouth, rubbed it against my jaw. "Ever had sex with anyone famous?" "No." "If so, who? If not, why not?" "Bad luck."

"Have you considered suicide?" "No."

I knew it might be the last time we met, so I drove him to my apartment, through the web of alleys around Mission and 11th, past Mark Bingham's office, now shuttered, dusty, and covered with dead flowers, a victim of the webcom bust and of course, a victim of terrorist cruelty. It's almost as if Al-Qaeda was targeting high tech, I thought, so furious with them. Not only Mark Bingham but Todd Beamer too, and everyone in first class who wasn't Muslim, who wasn't himself a terrorist, who didn't have those notes to study about how to die well—everyone on the plane who wanted to live. And what about the other plane on which Berry Berenson died? I hadn't known her myself but I had slept with her husband and I liked her, as one might like one's rival in a spirited game of gay rugby. "There's Bingham & Associates," I said to Dietmar Lutz. He told me I lived in a little toy part of town and the whole town's a toy and I'm still stuck being a toy man. "And here's where I live," I said.

"In your apartment."

"It's small," I warned him.

He made that clucking sound with his jaw as though to say, that figures. Dodie met us at the front door, make-up perfect, hair perfect. I watched her shake Dietmar's hand not betraying by a stir or shiver anything she might be feeling about him, there, on the threshold. The two cats, Blanche and Stanley, began sniffing his legs up to his knees. I recognized in their gesture a fellow feeling, the ecstasy of a stranger, how a stranger might resemble, might translate, into catnip; suddenly you're on your back with your paws in the air rubbing the back of your head into the carpet and not knowing why or caring why either. Just realizing that this is the event you've been waiting for perhaps your entire life. And to think that I learned this sorry lesson from a pair of cats, and from a German painter too, and of course from the teachings of terrorism! On the internet someone printed a collection of the scraps of paper found afterwards on the bodies of the terrorists of Flight 93. Little prayers and sayings. Instructions, pleas to Allah. Religious exhortations.

"Keep a very open mind, keep a very open heart of what you are to face. You will be entering paradise. You will be entering the happiest life, everlasting life. You will never enter paradise if you have not had a major problem. But only those who stood fast through it are the ones who will overcome it."

"Check all of your items—your bag, your clothes, knives, your will, your IDs, your passport, all your papers. Make sure that nobody is following you. . . . Make sure that you are clean, your clothes are clean, including your shoes."

"In the morning, try to pray the morning prayer with an open heart. Don't leave but when you have washed for the prayer. Continue to pray when you enter the plane: 'Oh God, open all doors for me. Oh God who answers prayers and answers those who ask you, I am asking you for your help. I am asking you for forgiveness. I am asking you to lighten my way. I am asking you to lift the burden I feel.'"

Dietmar brushed past us all, surveying the apartment, walking from room to room with his chin tilted up, his hands slightly away from his side, like an elderly hillbilly with a dowsing rod, until he found the place on the wall where the portrait would hang. "There," he said. Indicating a space of wall above the refrigerator. "Now let's begin."

Dodie's mouth moved to form the words I knew well. "How do I look?" I nodded reassurance and began to pose. "Like this? Like this?"

"Just be comfortable," Dietmar advised. "I'm going to take some photos." In digital sighs his silver camera took us apart and put us back together, refurbished.

"You are good for me," I told him. His camera blinked as I raised a can of Diet Pepsi up to my lips. "You are killing me."

"I'll leave the painting at the gallery," he said, packing his camera back into a neat little travel case. "Very nice to meet you, Dodie." With that he left our apartment and I ran out onto the landing with my car keys, offering to take him back to his room. "You don't give up," he said wryly. "You really make me sing for my supper, Kevin." We walked down Minna Street, around the corner to Lafayette, where the car was waiting by the deserted office Mark Bingham had once controlled. Flowers from admirers heaped up on the piss-stained pavement, flowers, American flags, the way they do when any accident causes a death in San Francisco. In the car I told Dietmar all about my theory of writing, but the more I got into it, the more confused my explanation grew. "Is it the purpose of writing to bring universal love to all the world? In writing, does one set down one's personal experience and hope that it strikes a universal chord in everyone?"

He snorted. The red bars flashed on his skin, down his cheeks. I missed a light; I was staring at them. "Listen to yourself, Kevin Killian. Substitute 'the United States' for 'writing' in all your pronouncements and you will see what's wrong with you, as an artist and a man."

"I wasn't the one who tried to conquer the world. That was you." Of course I meant the Germany of his Düsseldorf ancestors. "You deform me, you make me ugly."

"You *did* conquer the world," said Dietmar. "And now, see what is happening." Last I saw of him he was leaving my car, well, Dodie's car really, just him walking away briskly, his little Euro-case tucked under his arm.

Just as in love this illusion exists, this illusion of being able never to forget, so I was under the illusion that I would never forget Dietmar Lutz. City fathers tore down the Museum where I met him. Private developers reduced the house of Anton LaVey to rubble; on its site they plan to build some lofts. Dietmar's painting of me and Dodie hangs above our refrigerator just where he wanted it. I heard from him one last time, by email. "Just finished your portrait looking forward to the story. Dietmar."

HOT LIGHTS

For long stretches of time every day I kept my body inside my clothes, but sometimes it broke out and made a fool out of "me," the me I wanted to represent to the outside world. Hungry for heat and light, my body rolled itself out of hiding at the snap of a klieg light, and this scared me. It certainly ruined my chances for ever running for public office, and I suppose limited my options in other ways. For everything one's body does limits or directs the rest of one's future. I met Jig Johnson in the early seventies, when I was a college student, high as a kite but perpetually short on cash. Drugs were cheap then, so was liquor, but since I had only a job as a grocery clerk I was always on the make, trying to stay alive in New York. Four times a week I would sell my blood, traipsing from blood bank to blood bank all over midtown with a sprightly gait that tires me now just to think of it. A pal at school told me, sotto voce, of a man who paid students large sums for acting in porn loops. He said these loops, in primitive color, badly lit, could be seen in various raucous Times Square peep shows, where weirdos dropped a quarter in a slot and a lead shield shot up into the wall, unveiling a twist of naked limbs and cocks. At some random time, say, five minutes, the shield descended again implacably.

"Uh. . . ." "Duh. . . ." I weighed the pros and cons in my head like the figure of Libra on *Perry Mason.* Trying to figure out what would be right for me, but not thinking very clearly. I was naive to the nth degree. First of all, thanks to a steady diet of so-called "soft" porn, I didn't imagine that "acting" in porn would involve having sex in front of a camera. I had never actually seen a hard porn film. I had the suspicion that the actors might take off their clothes, might kiss, might pretend to have a kind of sex. Cynically I thought everything else was faked, as in Hollywood films. "Special effects." I remember, around that time, reading current discussions of gay representation in the media. I was taking "creative writing" at school, so I felt personally involved with the debate, and felt obliged to make all my gay characters positive images. Oh, amid what fog of delusion I walked Manhattan, straining my brains to think of ways to make everyone lovable . . . How would my appearance in a porn film affect the representation of my tribe? I couldn't work it out. When I called Jig Johnson from a public phone in the lobby of school, the line was busy so I went to my French class. After 90 minutes of Rimbaud and Verlaine I tried the number again. Ring. Ring. "Hello?" That's when I started to panic. Luckily Johnson was businesslike and really together, as if to compensate for the stupid qualms of the guys who were probably always calling him up to feed their habits. He asked me if I was ready to play with the big boys. "Sure." He asked if I was free that evening for my audition. There was a bottle of Southern Comfort in my pocket. Secretively I downed some, then sifted my little pile of thoughts like Brian Wilson playing in that sandbox. "What time?" I said, nodding out.

In his apartment he held my cock in his hands and watched it swell up, like one of those time-lapse photography miracles on public TV. I stared down too, feeling the simultaneous pride and shame of an unbidden erection. Presently, when I was hard as a bone, Johnson slapped my cock, told me to get down on my hands and knees on the floor. "Head on the side of the bed," he called out, from the other room, the room where my clothes were, I hoped. On the pinstriped gamy mattress, stained with a dozen men's come, I lay my head flat, praying I'd make it through my audition.

He dug a flash camera out of the hamper and dangled it close to my nose. God knows what I looked like, what distorted expression was frozen on my dumb face. Then the flash exploded and the chemical smell of the early Polaroid film filled the squalid room. As I remained there, stiff and blinking, he moved behind me to crouch down between my legs. I felt him trying to spread my knees, so I helped, trying to oblige. I don't know, did I do the right thing? I felt a wet hand slither down my butt, down its crack, and I wondered if he was going to screw me. I kept thinking, *I'm playing with the big boys now.*

But he told me he just wanted a picture of my asshole.

And there I was thinking, *What, no sex?* I remember being assaulted by my own thoughts and my feelings of unworthiness, while the Polaroid started to whirl. Presently he threw down two pictures in front of my face: grainy shots, in lurid color, of my demented face, and my tight little red hole, like a bullethole in the middle of what seemed an absurdly overstated butt.

"You'll be perfect," he said, and I wondered what perfection meant, if such banal evidences gave me so much pause. "You can dress now," he said, in a gentler tone. I covered my crotch with my hands as I walked out of the room. Like a little boy surprised. Suddenly I realized that porn acting involved actual sex captured on film. It just came to me in a revelation like St. Paul on the way to Damascus—a blinding light. "Far out," I thought, for I was always ready to have sex with other guys, but at the same time the thought of film's perpetuity unnerved me. It's one thing to reflect that, no matter how much of a mess she became, we can always think of Judy Garland as sweet sixteen singing in the cornfield; it was another to consider that, in a certain sense, I would always be a nineteen-year-old nitwit with a cock up my ass and a pot-induced glaze in my eyes. I found my clothes, undisturbed, and jammed them on willy-nilly. Johnson produced a bent card, with an address scribbled on the back. He tied my necktie for me, absently, helped me tuck in my shirt. He smelled of some lemony scent like the floor wax my mother used at home on her kitchen. He was indescribably dapper, everything I thought of when I thought of the words, "New York." Even the points of his collar were perfect white triangles, stiff, formal, like watercress sandwiches cut in half. I felt like a slob in front of him, could hardly look him in the eye. If I had, oh dear, what pity or contempt would I have seen there? Or was I his mirror, his younger self, a self without a single social grace, no ease? I steeled up my courage and insisted that I wouldn't play an effeminate hysterical hairdresser in his loop, a type gay activists were deploring in the great debate. "You won't be playing any type," he said—probably baffled. "You'll just be yourself." Swell, except I didn't know who that self could be. In looks I resembled a slightly beefed-up version of the Disney actress Hayley Mills—very androgynous, in the spirit of the times—and my voice had hardly broken, so I was still prone to embarrassing squeaks that made me wish the floor would open up. So—so whatever. . . .

At the front door another guy waited, in old army fatigues, and as if on a whim, Johnson had me unbutton the guy's pants and suck his cock for a minute. I thought about it for maybe ten seconds, then agreed, for auditioning had made me horny, and until this possibility of contact, I felt utterly unattractive. "Hi," the guy said. "Hmhhrw!" said I. He was my age, nineteen, or just about, with chalky white skin and hair dyed orange as Tropicana. I massaged his muscled thighs as I bobbed up and down in his lap. "That's fine," said Jig Johnson. "You can stop now." My co-star, whose name turned out to be Guy, shot a pitying glance at Johnson. "Where you recruiting now, Jig?" he said shakily. "Port Authority?" Johnson smiled and caressed Guy's orange sideburn in an absent avuncular manner, while Guy yawned and gradually reeled his dick back in his khakis. "There'll be six of you tomorrow," Johnson said. "Meet us at ten o'clock, Kevin."

"Okay," I stuttered, "and thanks, Mr. Johnson."

Guy called after me, "You're too good for this son of a bitch." Right then I kind of fell in love a bit. I set my alarm over and over again, took a dozen showers.

Of the actual filming I recall little. I mounted the stairs of a dilapidated building a block from Broadway—had the space once been a dance studio? Big quiet room, torn blinds drawn to the floor, a room scattered with the kind of furniture college students leave behind in their dorm rooms after they graduate. There was a steady roar in my head, a dull roar like a subway station, a roar which rose as I met my other co-stars and first saw the camera, a big box with a red light beaming underneath to show we were "on." Had they invented videotape back then? I don't think so. Here film itself was the precious, expensive thing, to be parceled out in stingy dear bits. I asked for my script, to give me something to read, to give me something to look at instead of all those distracting bodies sliding out of street clothes. I did notice that one guy had a shorter dick than mine, so I butched it up in all our scenes together; I'm no fool, I thought, *one less thing to obsess about.* . . .

"Jig, Kevin wants to take a look at the script." First a blank look, then a laugh, then everyone laughed at my naïveté. Guy, my co-star, patted my back consolingly, long white pats that brought the sweat dripping down into the crack of my ass. Nice guy. None of us had scripts per se, but there were scratch marks all over the carpet, drawn with chalk I suppose, of where we would stand at various intervals, usually down on one knee. Mystifying marks like the arbitrary symbols in the Lascaux caves. Johnson told us to make up all our dialogue, since another gang of boys would dub us over in a different situation, probably a different city. Everyone was hard, stiff, unbelievably so, and when the hot lights bore down on my erection it gleamed like topaz, under a light coating of mineral oil, and I said to myself, *I'd* take that home with me! *I'd* pay money to see that! *Who's* attached to this rod of steel?

It—my rod of steel—twitched, and great shadows leapt and fell across Guy's startled, tiny face underneath: he resembled a still from some excellent Maya Deren film like *Meshes of the Afternoon.*

One guy, Charles, long blond hair like Fabio's, touch of a blond goatee at the base of his spine, spent hours bent over the back of a large sofa, getting fucked over and over, and his only line was "Mount me,"—*that* stuck with me. In the morning his asshole was a thin slit, moist, exquisitely puckered, but by late afternoon it looked like a red rubber ball, torn in half and pierced with blood, sunk deep within. Most of all I remember the heat of the lights, how huge lights two feet wide threatened to blow the fuses of the entire apartment building, and how when their shutters opened a giant click sound rocked the whole room. These white-hot domes, trained on one's skin, were like the great eyes of God the poet Jack Spicer wrote of in *Imaginary Elegies.* They see everything, even under the skin where your thoughts are. Your dirty little thoughts. You can take off all your clothes and pretend to be "naked," but you are still Kevin Killian from Smithtown, Long Island, with all the petty details that denotes. And yet at the same time the heat made me feel languorous, forgetful, like Maria Montez at the top of some Aztec staircase—dangerous, as though there were nothing beyond the circle of white—no audience, no society, only oneself and the red or purple or black hard-on that floats magically to the level of one's lips. I suppose all actors must feel the same way in some part of being—that the camera's eye represents the eye of God, which at the same time judges all and, threateningly, withholds all judgment till time turns off.

We poured out onto the street at sunset, tired and spent, yakking it up. We would never be stars, I thought. No one would ever see this "loop." And I was glad, but sorry too. I asked if anyone knew the name of the picture. No one did. (Charlie said they should call it *Saddlesore*.) It didn't really have a name, and as such, I thought, it had no real existence. Just six guys fucking and sucking. We said we would all meet in six months at a Times Square grindhouse for the premiere. Auld acquaintance. I tried visualizing our putative audience and words popped into my head: "a bunch of perverts"—shady men in black trenchcoats, visiting conventioneers touring the louche side of gay New York. Nobodies, in fact. "Bye, dudes." "Later." "Adios." I took away more money than I'd ever made in my life—a hundred dollars, except Johnson took back like three dollars because he bought us some lunch—beer and Kentucky Fried Chicken. At the same time I read some interview with Lou Reed: asked whether he thought homosexuality was increasing, he replied to the effect that, "It's a fad, but people will tire of it, because eventually you have to suck cock or get your ass fucked." I reflected that I had in one fell swoop ruined my chance to be president, earned $97.00, made a new boyfriend, kind of, solidified my connections with the entertainment world, had some great sex, and still I felt utterly ashamed of my own specularity, my need to see and be seen. I came, onto the face and chest of a boy, and my semen seemed to spatter and fry, before my eyes, as though his body were the very skillet of love, such was the wattage of those hot lights.

I remember walking around Columbus Circle looking for things to buy with my money, and feeling disappointed there are no stores there, only pretzel vendors and hot dog carts, so I bought a pretzel and a hot dog, and stood with one foot curled around the ironwork fence at Central Park South, watching the crowd. Wondering if anyone could "tell." My wallet felt fat, expansive, as though my money might grow to enormous size and eat the whole fucking city. I was so filled up with energy I thought I could walk all the way uptown to Guy's neighborhood, then just kind of drop in, rekindle our newfound intimacy, lick that dead-white skin from the nape of his neck to the puncture wounds inside his arm. . . .

I slid into a bar on Sixth Avenue, pondering desire, Guy, money and guilt. Had I let down my tribe by playing a part which wasn't actually a part per se, but couldn't therefore be a "positive" one? Wish I could go back and console my younger self, rub his young shoulders, explicate latter-day porn theory to cheer him up. And also get him to cut back on all that drinking! At once the most and least ironic of art forms, pornography undercuts the performative authenticity of penetration with oh, just lashes of mad camp. Its greatest stars, like those of performance art, are the biggest dopes in the world; its most discerning fans those, like my present-day self, who feel ourselves beyond representation for one imaginary reason or another. I stepped into a liquor store on 82nd for a bottle of Seagram's 7, knowing I'd find an answer in its rich musky depths. On the way out I saw a phone booth, and I called Guy, who had scrawled his number backwards up my thigh from the back of my knee to the juncture of my balls. "I know it's not six months yet," I said, "but I was thinking—"

"I can still taste your dick in my mouth," he said—an encouraging sign, or so I thought, but instead he hung up on me, and I felt a blush rise right up to my temples. I thought everyone was staring at the dumb boy on the dumb phone who just got the brush-off. The glare of judgment burning me like lasers through my cool.

I kept thinking, I'm wearing way too many clothes! And I fled. Finally night fell and I looked up at the moon that shone over Morningside Heights, its white soft beam so limpid, full of the poetry of Shakespeare and the Caribbean and George Eliot—the antithesis I suppose of the hot lights I had grown to need. How relaxed, how relieved I now felt, in the white moonlight. Relieved of the chore of playing with the big boys. My clothes seemed to fit again, I became myself. The moon's fleecy lambency corralled my pieces and re-linked us, we joined "hands" as it were and sang and danced in a circle, very Joseph Campbell, "me" regnant, manhood ceremonial. Birth of the hero. I became Kevin Killian. Did I make a mistake?

WHITE ROSE

for Clifford Hengst

The doctor's waiting room, which was very small, was almost full when I entered, bleeding from my right arm. After speaking to the nurse, I stood by the magazine table, sizing up the seating situation with a steady expressionless gaze. There was no air. I waited a few minutes, studying a young man who sat in the next chair, his legs crossed, a slick magazine in his lap. "Scratch 'n' sniff," he said with a grin. When I peered over, I saw his hard dick, about a yard long, inching up the open magazine between his legs—*Field and Stream*, if I remember correctly. He winked at me, opened his red mouth, and let his tongue loll out one side. I stood up and told the nurse to cancel my appointment.

"I thought it was an emergency," she clicked in reproof. "That's a bad cut you got on your arm there."

Two options lay open to me: I could have had my arm seen to, bandaged up, or I could take the boy in the chair somewhere and suck his cock. He was not a bad-looking young man though he had on a bright blue suit and yellow socks that were not pulled up far enough. He had prominent face bones and a streak of sticky-looking blonde hair falling across his forehead. He beamed at me, pointing to his magazine and what it contained. I crossed back to where he lounged, ordered him to go with me.

Told him I'd take care of his problem.

"Suit yourself," sniffed Nurse Ratched.

I followed the boy out into the lot—late summer, the sun slamming us in the face. The tar shimmered with jets and stars of black, looked like melting water under our feet. I couldn't take my eyes off the small of his back as he swaggered in front of me, peeling off the jacket to his bright blue suit. He was a white boy, just under six feet tall, with a big red Dodge pickup gleaming in the afternoon sun. In the countryside, fifty miles west of Atlanta, nearly everyone's got a pickup and most of them are red. He jiggled the keys, cocked a lean hip against the red-hot hood. The zipper to his suit pants was still undone, but I couldn't really see anything now, for the sun slanting hungrily into his crotch, was far too bright. "Let's ride some," he said. "When we get to where we're going you can take care of my problem."

I slid in beside him, asked his name, what county he came from. "You're not from around here," he told me. "Everyone knows me who lives here in Milledgeville. Call me Eric." The cab was strewn with old beer cans, fried chicken pieces, shotgun shells, and cash. The radio tuned to some local country station, Randy Travis, George Strait. He grabbed my left hand and undid his seat belt, shoving my hand into the tight space between the seat covers and his butt, so he could sit on it as he drove out of town.

"You like that?" he asked. He kept compressing, then releasing, all the muscles in his butt, so I could feel the whole area with my good hand. "I knew early on I was never gonna be the kind of boy my Mama and Daddy wanted me to be. I got married, got kids, but that's far as I go in their direction." I envied him his courage. Felt a bit sorry for his kids and wife, but hey, life's a bitch. In the meantime I had but one mission in life, to get into that perfect little ass. Eric chucked off his blue wool necktie, tossed it back into the cab, and unbuttoned the first three buttons of his soft white cotton shirt. On the radio the news announcer told us that the "Misfit" had broken out of the state pen in Angola and was seen heading for Georgia. I pushed the button, off. Eric pushed it back on. He said, "There's just one thing I don't do, I don't get fucked." Okay, I thought, that's fair speaking, but I'll teach you to like it, Mr. Eric-with-the-blue suit. I'll teach you to beg for it like a seal.

After ten miles and two beers apiece, Eric pulled the Dodge off-road into a clearing set in the middle of a patch of ironweed, under a big tree with branches that reached halfway to the pale, flat sky. He slammed his door and walked around to mine, like he was going to open it up for me, like I was some lady friend of his, maybe his wife. I opened his pants and tugged them down to his hips. Underneath he wore a pair of tangled Fruit of the Looms, tangled with his cock, half in, half out, like a briar rose. He was embarrassed, he said, cause his dick wasn't big enough, not really. I said it was fine. I leaned forward, put my mouth round its head, felt it swell up, big as a plum, sweeter; then

I grabbed the funky underwear apart, so I could cup his balls in my greedy palms. I felt something rip, the sound of cotton splitting apart. I grabbed me a cute chunk of his butt and pulled, squeezed, while I dipped his cock deeper in my mouth, tasted its wiry freshness and sweetness. He patted my hair, like he was starting to panic. "Boy," I told Eric, "you were bold in the doctor's office, but you're one scared rabbit, ain'tcha." I like 'em kind of scared, like they never done this before. His pubic hair was red and gold, felt like it was on fire as it scratched my face, and his dick got hard in my mouth, my tongue teasing at the long blue vein on its underside. My tongue could feel that vein pumping up and down like a wild pulsebeat. "I don't want to come," he said. "Boy, you're gonna come," I said, like it was an order.

He grabbed my shoulders and the old pain in my right arm flared up, opening the knife wound. Blood began to trickle down my arm, soaking through my gray prison overall. His eyed widened but I glared up at him, his cock rock-hard in my mouth, and maybe that's when he started putting two and two together about the Misfit's prison break. I dabbled some blood from the long cut that serrated my bicep, smeared it along his dick, then gobbled it down. "Yeah, baby," he moaned. "Make me come all over your face." I was still sitting sideways on the passenger seat, my jaws full up with his works. Again and again he thrust that skinned man meat down my hungry, burning throat while I swooned a hundred times. His big balls banged against my chin, I tried tickling them from underneath with bloody fingers. "I'm a hard come, Misfit," he wheezed. "Quick," he cried, "put something up my butt. Your finger or whatever."

Without thinking I brought out the snub-nosed .38 out from under the seat of the pickup. I parted his heaving butt cheeks and mounted its cool nose right there at Eric's tiny wrinkled hole. "Scratch 'n' sniff," I grunted. He knew what it was, all right. His blue eyes grew wide, his balls grew heavy and tight, and he unleashed a furious volley of cum down my throat like a firehose. "Christ almighty!" he hollered. "You are one sick son of a bitch there, son, come on, now, come on and fuck me!" I milked his silky pulsating dick for all it was worth, then wiped my mouth on his thigh and plucked the gun out of his ass, slid it in my pocket. He stared at me with the stupid happy vacant gaze of one who's shot the biggest load of his young career. He dressed again, found his keys, and we took off down 217 towards Marietta. Kid. A kid who wouldn't have been so bad if someone had been there to stick a gun up his ass, then pulled the trigger, every day of his life.

"Where we goin'?" he asked.

"Just shut up and keep towards the right," I replied.

My arm was hurting me again. I ordered him to rip up that soft white shirt of his, bind my arm with the pieces.

"I like doing it in the woods," Eric said hopefully. "You feel more free here, not all cooped up." By the side of the road a patch of marigold peeked out from the underbrush, bright orange in a snarl of brittle thorn branches.

"We're not goin' to no woods," I told him. "And hey, Eric, I'd appreciate a little manual stimulation right about now."

"On your arm?" he said.

I shot him a withering glance.

"Oh yeah," he said. "I'm gonna let that big rod of yours

be my stick shift." His hand touched my cock through the rough fabric of the coverall. Don't think he knew what the Lord had in store for him. His hand kept traveling, perplexed, finger by finger like the Yellow Pages ad. He couldn't find the end of it. I said, "Just grab on to what you can, my friend. And that, incidentally, should be your motto for life."

I made him pull over to a barn-like structure just outside Marietta. It was a place I had brought many men, young and old, black and white. No one had been by for many years, but it was the house where I was born, now covered with the cobwebs and mildew of disuse. In the loft above the barn the sun had cooked the pine boards to well done. Smooth pine, like the inside of a coffin. He peered out the dusty window, tried to tug it open a bit, but it was stuck fast. I slipped up behind him and crossed my thick sunburnt hands around his little old waist. "Don't," he said, scared, backing into me, so that his hindquarters brushed against my hard-on. The layers of cloth between us infuriated me, the heat blinded me. Blind and hot with impatience, I ripped the thin belt off his pants and smacked it on the floor. His pants sagged past his hips, and the cheeks of his white ass leaned out like two friendly pups lookin' for affection. I could see the tight ass crack, luscious, like a promise of greatness. His hands flapped in space as I pulled his bright blue pants down to the dusty pine floor. "Bend over for Papa," I whispered to him. Dust—particles of bright dust, dazzling—fell and bounced from the bare wood floor beneath my boots. Christ, was it hot! Felt like we were two chickens roasting in a broiler. Naked but for his yellow socks, Eric grew skittery, his easy Southern charm beginning to fade at the edges. "I told you, I don't like nothing anal," he sighed, bent over, ass up in the dusty air.

Two low red patches sat on the cheeks of his butt. Otherwise that little fidgety ass was completely white, satiny, like a white rose. The shadow of down that outlined his crack, and the sweat that glazed it, looked like pollen in the shadowy heat, pollen attracted to the sweet heat of his asshole. A fly zigzagged in lazy loops through the air between us. I raised my hand, sucked on my fingers, one by one. I could smell his fear. "What're you gonna do with me?" he said, a tremor in his voice.

"I always wonder," I snapped.

"You're the Misfit . . . aren't you?" said he. I sucked on his shoulder blade, felt around a bit, my left arm extended to his cock and balls, squeezed them like a sponge dipped in his water. He grew in my hands, then he grabbed himself with his own hands, anxious to keep hard. I studied the twin globes of flesh beneath me, then applied my wet fingers to his firm buns, and pulled them open like curtains. Inside the crack, lined with blonde fuzz, I saw his moist rose-colored hole, staring back at me, afraid, like all of us, of the open air; and I put one finger on top of it, slid it up and down, felt it twitch. Scared. "Don't hurt me none, now, Misfit," he said with a low voice.

"If I decide to, I'll let you know," I replied. "And if I do, you'll enjoy that too. Because I am the mouth of the South."

The fly dropped to the dusty floor and we watched it expire—of heat, I suppose: heat and thirst. He trembled. One drop of sweat trickled down from the nape of his neck, and seeped over his shoulder blade, stopping on a freckle a few inches above his waist. Then, as I gazed in wonder, the entire surface of his bare back broke out into a shimmering mist of sweat, translucent and clear, like the fog that hovers over the lowlands right after dawn in late summer. I plunged one finger up his ass, up to the second knuckle. He yelped, drew forward, hard, like he's been burnt, and hit his head on the wall like a damn fool. I twisted my finger round and round, inside the warm red asshole, its lips the same red color as his mouth. They moved like his mouth, with an inadvertent smirk. Another finger shot up, through the wet ring, and I began to rotate the fingers in his butt like I was dialing a number on an old rotary telephone. The kind of phone everyone used to have when I first went to Angola.

Eric wriggled and jiggled under my pressure, moaning and squirming like a little boy. I pulled my hard cock free of my overall, and it leaped up at the sight of my fingers—three of them now, rough and callused from hard labor—working inside that greasy red asshole. Yes, it fair jumped up like a snake, ready to bite that boy's plush soft interior. Sharply I slapped one cheek of his ass. "What you in the doctor's office for, boy?" I said.

No answer, just more pressure round my wiggly fingers. I smelled his sweat on me, his sweat and stink. I slapped him again, harder, saw the pink flush rise up on his skin in the exact print of my hand. He made no answer, just little grunts and moans you couldn't even call English, but I ain't picky. I jammed my thumb up his writhing hole, told him to talk.

"AIDS test," he said presently, peering up at me over

his tanned shoulder, that greasy lock of blonde hair flapping over his eyes. Staring at me as if to say, *you ast for it, Misfit.* I wanted to fuck him more than I ever wanted to fuck another human being in my life. He reached for his pants, which I'd kicked across the hot pine floor, and pulled out a rubber all wrapped in foil. I made Eric open it with his teeth, then slapped it up and over the first part of my straining hot cock. "Please don't fuck me," he said. Aw, I bet he said that to all the fellas in Milledgeville.

"I need you to tell me you don't have AIDS."

"Swear to God I don't," he cried. "Where's the gun, for God's sake?"

So I withdrew my hand and looked right up his gaping red butthole, begging for it. What had once been a tight, virginal rosebud was now, after lube after lube of spit, sweat and elbow grease, almost wide enough to accommodate me. He groaned with anticipation, saying, "I've got money, Misfit."

"That I knew right off," I whispered. "This is a class thing after all." With one sharp thrust I entered him, yowling that I was gonna commit murder, and he crashed to his knees, me still inside him, my mighty arms hugging his skinny ribs. Inside Eric was hotter and wetter than any pussy in the world—and he knew it too. "That's it, Daddy," he howled, scrabbling on the dusty floor, while I kept fucking him with long steady strokes, strokes that scraped the lining of his guts and glands. "Kill me with that big motherfuck dick of yours." His yellow socks bobbed in the air as his feet kicked under mine. I slammed his head to the floor. God, did his white butt feel good eating my dick like candy. Clear pearly beads of sweat, his and mine both, commingled, came sluicing down his bare back, flowing down between his ripe ass cheeks, right into the space where his hole was stopped up by my big stiff woody. Sweet sensation bucked and bounced along the throbbing length of my dick, buried deep inside him, and the little hot cherry gland right under my balls. "I'm a hard come, Eric Blue Suit," I told him. "You and me could keep this up an hour or more."

"Oh, God," he called out. "Fuck me, man, hard now, harder."

"We could stay here till sunup, but I need this one thing to pull my trigger."

"Oh, God," he said. "What is it, Daddy?"

"Tell me you've never done this before."

"I—" He tried to speak, but I put one big meaty hand over his red lips, pressed down, felt his tongue and teeth trying to talk.

"Tell me I'm the first man who put his dick up your ass."

He kept nodding, frantic, but couldn't speak—not with my fist jamming his throat. His eyes grew wider and wider, till they resembled two wild jewels, but he couldn't speak. I kept fucking him, managed to switch on his prostrate. His poor worn out dick stood straight out, dark red, almost purple, and a big grin came to his face, a grin I could feel through my fist. My cock filled to bursting point, swollen by the uncountable contractions of his asshole muscles. "Tell me what I want to hear," I called down to him.

"You're the first, the only," he mumbled, his eyes closed now as the seed flowed from him, shot out into the narrow space between his body and the floor. Yes! Yes! My dick exploded in a series of mighty paroxysms. The dusty, hot loft vanished, and we were whirling in space together, a space without prisons, class, money, or whatever. Like a comet out of the heavens I came and came, up the narrow channel of his butt, a river in full flow. Then, still inside him, I took his head and swiveled it round so I could gaze into his blue eyes, face to face. And I knew he was lying at me. . . . All would have been fine and dandy if he hadn't lied at me. . . .

after Flannery O'Connor

ROCHESTER

I should have called first. If I were in an airplane I would see a cross-section of streets that connect and disconnect at odd, inorganic angles. But I'm not in an airplane and from an aerial view I must look like a dope, limping the wrong way down a one-way street, lugging an overnight bag filled with souvenirs. (Yes, I went shopping. Had to buy poor Tim Baker *something* —I got him a light bulb refrigerator magnet that says "Rochester, the City of Light"—and then I saw some Beanie Babies which Gregory collects like mad and he doesn't have these—cute little inchworm, cute little chimp, etc. So there I was with a bag stuffed with animals stuffed with beans. And a dream in my head.) Navigation has never been my strong suit. According to someone—you know, the "they say" of undisputed fact—men are supposed to have a more powerful sense of direction than women, who in turn are more likely to remember landmarks in lieu of "north" and "south." Well, I must be a woman trapped in a man's body, because I'm pretty much lost, looking for—what? All the houses look the same: early-twentieth-century duplexes with classic Southern porches. Chipped paint. Couple fighting. I'm in crackville. Then I spot it, the dilapidated corner store, and know I'm getting close. Kevin has told me he goes there to get the daily draw.

And now, at last, Kevin Killian limps out onto his porch, his face a haggard blur of lines. "You Tony?" he grunts. He's been sewing, he explains, a new apron. That's how he spends his days, apparently: sewing old rags together to make new garments to wear around the house. He never goes out, almost never leaves his living room. I'm wondering, my God, how old is he? And when did he write those books that I read, long ago, in San Francisco?

"I'm forty-five," he blurts out, extending a hand to me as I climb up on the porch. "Welcome to Rochester." For a minute I lose track of consciousness and mistake his meaning, thinking of him as the ruined Rochester of Bronte's *Jane Eyre*, the Gothic hero in decline. Then I come to, with a snap, the kind of snap produced when one walks across a floor strewn with that plastic bubble wrap I used to gather together in San Francisco and make visual art masterpieces out of—in my other career, the artist. I'm here as a writer. A young poet come to make the acquaintance of the strange "Wizard of Rochester."

From inside the house I hear the enthusiastic bang bang click click of someone using an old-fashioned electronic typewriter, really whizzing away. I wonder, does someone else live in this house? I always know Gregory's home since Céline Dion is usually blasting away how near, far, wherever I am, her heart will go on. But now I keep hearing the ringing repeated as typist X reaches the end of the line again and again, has to hit the carriage return. Someone is writing faster than most people think.

I met Kevin Killian online. I was over Tim Baker's house in the Castro district; we'd just come back from the Midnight Sun. The "Sun" as we call it. It was after three o'clock and the streets were streaked with black rain and the slithery sequins of night. In Tim's apartment a silvery box hummed and moaned. "I'm on alt.weird.Rochester," he said—first indication I had that he was into the Goth thing, and I'm thinking, maybe I should bail, that is so over, especially in the Castro. But every time I bail on somebody, I acquire an overwhelming sense of guilt. And it ain't pretty. It's as if I wake up with three added layers of fat around my gut, only the fat is in my head. I'm losing track, I suppose. What I'm trying to say is if I bailed on Goth boy I would have never met Kevin Killian.

When I stumbled onto Kevin in a dirty chatroom, I thought it was mere coincidence, that somebody shared his name. In time, however, I learned that Kevin Killian was indeed Kevin Killian, a great writer now condemned to live in Rochester, NY, teaching at a small local community college all because of some unnamed indiscretion years ago.

Through email, Kevin proved himself a reliable correspondent. I could have done without the forwarded news flashes from the Sally Field Fan Club—though even these I saved as proof of my connection to this great man. As I step onto his porch, shake his hand, he takes a tottering step back, almost knocking over a silver milkbox filled with glass empties. God, in *San Francisco,* we don't even have glass milk bottles any more . . . If we *ever* did! I'll have to ask somebody really old like Armistead Maupin. Or Tim Baker might know, he must be thirty-two or thirty-three and this complete retard socially. He's not exactly the kind you'd bring to the Black and White Ball . . . he's okay. . . .

Spitting out his cigarette Kevin Killian tells me to turn around, as if to point out the view from his porch—the view of decaying Rochester. I comply.

"You got a good ass."

I don't know what to say.

"Wanna fuck?"

My eyes bulge.

He laughs. "Just kidding kid, I always try that one on the turd who cuts my grass. Come on in, come see the accoutrements of a life devoted to writing, poetry, poverty, jouissance, and high art. How old are you, Tony Leuzzi? Twelve? Thirteen?"

I pause at the threshold, relieved, of course, but also a bit peeved, wishing I had my pocket mirror. Do I really look twelve? I don't think so. The reason Gregory went for me in the first place is my build. A swimmer's body he says. "I don't want to bother whoever's typing," I say, gingerly crossing the threshold.

Killian snorts. "You won't bother him. That's Chester."

He stops, starts again. "Nothing bothers ol' Chester."

Inside the house I make out a few dim shapes, pieces of furniture from a bygone day: chesterfields, hutches, Victorian bric-a-brac, and a pair of feral-looking cats, their eyes glowing in the dark, staring back at me. The smell's indescribable, but I'll try . . . a sour, fetid smell, as though clothes had gone bad in a hamper. Overlaid, another smell, ripe fruit, bananas, papayas? I look back over my shoulder. The novelist stands there, courteously urging me further in. Is this what Jeffrey Dahmer's victims felt like during their last glimpse of the outside world?

Goodbye sunlight, goodbye fresh air, goodbye to California . . . and hello Rochester, the cloistered claustrophobic world of things gone mad from inertia and prodigal disuse. Killian must notice my hesitation, because I feel a sharp pain in my right my right hip; he's pushed a sharpened screwdriver against the back pocket of my jeans. Jeans Gregory bought me in San Francisco to mark our one-year anniversary of being a couple. As I stumble into the dark hallway, I rub myself for good luck. Oh well! I've been brave enough to leave the City to seek a mentor, and I can't complain if I come out of this with no more than a bizarre pass made on me by no less than a living legend.

"Want some applesauce?" he says, indicating the kitchen and, on a plain deal table, an open jar of yellow, viscous pulp. "We grow the apples round back, then mash them in the tub. I got to wash this Phillips driver. You eat some applesauce." He crosses to the sink—a large sixteen-gallon tin sink mounted on the wall with wire and duct tape—and flicks on the tap. Rusty water pours over his hands and slides off the arrowhead tip of the screwdriver.

"Okay," I reply.

"Okay, what?"

"Okay, I'll have some applesauce."

"You really want that shit?"

"Well, uh, I was *trying* to be polite."

"You could have been just as polite and said 'no,' right?"

"I'm not really hungry anyway."

"Where did that come from?"

"What—"

"Man, you're a doe-in-the-headlights. Wait here. Be right back."

I wait exasperated and vaguely humiliated in his closet-sized kitchen for what seems like an eternity. I have time to run my finger along the filmy Formica countertop, study the pattern in the peeled-back linoleum, and try to get acquainted with one of the cats. The feline will have none of it.

"Hey, jail bait, look up and say 'guilty'!"

I'm too stunned to respond to the sudden flash. He said guilty. I thought of the cat. Only afterward did I realize he was holding a Polaroid camera the size of China in his right arm. The thing looked older than me. Must have been an early model.

"Gotcha!"

"Thanks a lot."

"Oh, don't get offended. I mean you do look like a moron, but still. Here, look."

I see a freshly exposed image of myself in a square about four inches wide, four inches long. I don't look like a moron at all. I'm very fresh-faced, with short curly dark hair and smooth skin touched with the sea foam of my native land. My teeth are white, my tongue protrudes slightly from one corner of my sensual mouth. My eyes are black and I'm convincingly slim. I've got a swimmer's body. "I'll do better when I'm not surprised," I say, sour applesauce glugging down my throat. "You shocked me."

"Fair's fair," he says. He hobbles to the huge Victorian desk and throws a pad of yellow legal paper at me. "Write something, Tony. Write anything."

"Okay," I reply.

"Okay, what?"

"Okay, I will."

"Okay, Mr. Killian," he snaps back, bending over to pet one of the two enormous cats who come crawling over his black high-laced boots. "You want to write, we'll write, but we'll do it my way, naked."

Luckily I have brought my laptop for just such an occasion. He glimpses it warily as I unpack it from out of my Versace gym bag. Gregory bought me the bag to mark our eighteen-month anniversary as a couple. The laptop gleams like a polished slab from another, silicon-based planet. Behind me Kevin Killian's breathing stertorously, as though he'd never seen a computer in his life (which I know's untrue, since I met him in a "chat room"—the virtual world in which asshole me thought he was someone of stature. God! I'd never heard of him but Tim Baker, the librarian from hell, told me about him, trying to interest me in something so I'd find him interesting himself, as though I'd ever do him when he knows I'm involved very romantically with Gregory who's half his age and extremely sweet and giving. *Poor Tim Baker! When you're five-foot-five and covered with extra body hair and sport thick glasses with smeary lenses, and then someone like me kind of feels sorry for you, the Castro must be a strange kind of purgatory).* And so now Kevin Killian's standing there, tapping his toe, and I can't get the cursor blinking. Must be something in the electrical field around Rochester. "Do I have to be naked?" I stammer, as I sit down at the table and pull the legal pad toward me.

"No," he says shortly. "I've seen it all in every JPEG that ever came out of San Fran-fucking-cisco. I want you to tell me about your soul. So write it all down and meanwhile I'll make you some applesauce that'll burn the roof of your mouth off. Just let me put the finishing touches on this here apron first. By the way, I took a message for you. From a Gregory?"

"That's my lover," I tell him.

"He says he misses you already. And then I got an e-mail for you, from a Tim Baker."

"Oh." I'm rolling my eyes. "He's this persistent frump in the Castro who does my taxes. Some guys think if they just stare at you long enough, mournfully enough, you'll magically lie on your back and lift your knees in the air. That's the Tim Baker story."

But he's bent over the apron so I don't feel my words are too important. I scoot back into the chair, bending over the legal pad. I try to write something, anything, so that I don't feel like a fraud. Nothing, however, will come. I don't know if the problem is that I'm no longer used to writing in longhand or if I'm scared to death of what this crazed man will say.

He wants me to write about my soul. I don't even know what that is. I've been writing for a few years on some impulse to represent what I see around me. While I'm sure my writing is connected with my soul, I haven't really spent all that much time focusing on interior stuff—for lack of a better term—since I don't even know what to call it.

Oh, God, this is the same problem I've had with every one of my boyfriends in the last couple years: "You don't know what you want, you don't know what you feel. . . ." they always say. I pass off such talk as psychobabble and mock them ruthlessly for emoting all the time. But maybe, just maybe, they were right after all.

I write the first thing that comes to mind:

"Many say that I'm too young, to let you know just where I'm coming from. . . ."

And I like it until I realize that it isn't mine. It's a line from Aretha Franklin's "Giving Him Something He Can Feel," which I heard on the bus this morning, booming from somebody's ghetto blaster. I cross the sentence out and think again. Okay, here it goes:

"The hounds are snoring in the caverns of my restless brain."

Good. Fine. Wonderful. I like it. Immensely. Though I'm not really sure how to follow it up. At this point, I hear mashing sounds coming from the bathroom. Oh, for a minute I forgot I was in Killian's house. He's making me applesauce. I better write more. And the typing has gone on, without a pause, for the past twenty minutes. I'm sitting here with the worst writer's block in the world, and someone's writing *War and Peace* right in the next room, terrific. Marvelous. For this I left San Francisco?

"I want to show you something," Killian says abruptly, barging into the kitchen again.

He hands me a piece of typing paper completely filled up with characters. Meaningless. Here and there a circle of red magic marker surrounds a random group of letters. "Look," he says, "what does this word say?"

"Car," I reply.

"And this?"

"Diana," I read off the shaky paper floating in front of my face.

"And this?"

"Die," I say. "Is it about Princess Diana?"

He nods. "When I first spotted this one, I thought Diana was going to kill someone in a car. I didn't know that she'd be killed herself. Syntax! Syntax is missing. Look, here's another. This I got in 1988."

He presents me with another sheet of paper, likewise filled with meaningless combinations of numbers, typographical signs, and alphabetical characters. Again, three red circles triumphantly signal a few English words. "Tonie"—"eat"—"apple." Rather, "aPpLE." "When you sent me that email, said you were coming, I remembered this page, looked it up in my concordance." He points at a bulging loose-leaf binder open—so stuffed with paper it can't be closed—on a low table in the corner. "And then I went down to the cellar and found the page. So when you came, I made you eat the apple."

"I don't spell my name with an i-e at the end," I say rather coldly. "Say, what is this, anyhow?"

"Here's another one," he says, as though I haven't asked a question. Obediently I read the words that showed up in the red circles. "Ski." "Sonny." "Die." "Tree."

I stare at Kevin Killian, who stared back at me as though trying not to laugh. His thin lips recessed over his prominent gums.

"I get it," I say. "It's about Sonny Bono, right?"

"Yep, and check out the date, kid."

"1985."

"April, 1985," he says. "Conclusive?"

"Of what?"

"Of writing," he breathes. He comes closer, I smell the faint traces of bananas on his long, twitchy fingers. I feel at this instant he is going to grab me. On instinct, I jump out of my chair—clumsily of course—and skitter to the other side of the table like a trapped rat.

"What's your game?"

"I don't play games with people."

"Oh, yeah? Well what's all this shit about? You've been trying to fuck with my head, not to mention my ass, ever since I walked through that door!"

"Your anger is interesting," Kevin replies, and smiles knowingly. Rather calmly, he continues: "It says a lot about you. It says that you have become your own worst enemy. Your own censor. Your own danger." In the other room, the typing continues.

"Hey, now, you're the one who's been making moves on me—"

"Is that what you call it?" He laughs harshly. "You've been selling your sex appeal over the net for years and I'm the one who's out of line? I've just been giving you what you have wanted all along. A reason to get mad. You're a very troubled young man. I've known this for some time. Long before I met you. You could say," he says unctuously, "that my writing told me."

"I— You— What?—" In a second's flash I bolt past him towards that mysterious door. The typing is relentless now, and when I open it I see something that makes my sweating feet totter precariously on the edge of my shoes.

Sitting behind the typewriter, and typing away furiously, is a full-size, if not overgrown, chimpanzee! Must be four feet tall, and its paws or whatever they are pound away at the keyboard like six people typing at once. When it sees me, it stops for a minute, surveys me cursorily with large, lustrous black eyes, then seems to dismiss me, pausing only to peel the tough yellow outer skin from a banana with surprising skill.

"That's Chester," says Kevin Killian, behind me.

You'd think the room in which a filthy man keeps a chimp caged would be filthy itself, but strangely enough, it's just the opposite. Chester's room has a neatness, a freshness about it at odds with the rest of the house. Later, Kevin tells me that "Chester" keeps himself astonishingly clean and even uses the toilet like a human being. "He likes beige and white. They soothe him." There are few pictures, only a color reproduction of a Nan Goldin photograph clipped from an old issue of *Artforum*. There's a neat, tiny shelf of Kevin Killian's books on the wall above "Chester's" office chair. There's the desk, a typewriter, the chair, and in the corner, neatly made up, is Chester's little bed, with a headboard made out of willow. The room smells sweet. Chester keeps typing.

"Writing comes out of the beyond," Kevin says. "Little by little, it comes to Chester. And then I get it, and I cross out some words and publish it as my own."

"That thing wrote all your books?"

I'm stammering.

"Yes, and now he's writing a new novel for me. As well as predicting my future and yours."

The chimp rips a page out of the carriage and jumps

onto the padded seat of his office chair, holding the page up above its hairy head with great excitement.

Kevin yanks at my belt, sharply. "He's overexcited," he whispers in my ear. "Tell me—did you bring any monkey simulacra with you into this house?"

"Why—no," I falter. "Unless you mean—"

Chester jumps down from the chair and walks over to me. His huge hands start patting my ankles, and calves, and knees, probingly, searchingly. He drops the finished page onto the polished hardwood floor.

"He's looking for his double," Kevin says. "That's what I'm always looking for too. I'm looking for my own reflection every time I meet a new friend."

"At the airport—no, at the bus station," I tell him, "I bought a couple of Beanie Babies for my boyfriend. For Gregory. One of them's a chimp."

"There you have it! Better get it now, otherwise Chester will be searching your body forever, and who knows, you might get to like it." Indeed the indefatigable animal has one massive paw across my crotch at this very moment. The other arm is probing in the back pocket of my jeans.

I guess I could get to like the feeling. Reminds me of the time I was over Tim Baker's house, and he had just finished doing my taxes, and I guess I had had a few too many hits off the bong and fell asleep, and when I woke up, Tim Baker had my pants down off my hips and was rubbing my dick with his mouth.

Wasn't really a blow job, just kind of a—I don't know—caress. . . .

I bend down and retrieve the paper, while Kevin's in the front room looking through my gym bag for Gregory's

Beanie Baby, and Chester stares at me with those huge black eyes, his mouth slightly open, as though he had a message of inestimable value to impart.

I'm not sure what I'm feeling. I'm thinking back to Tim Baker's pathetic little room, and my sleeping there, with the reassuring sound of his calculator clicking and clacking away. Gregory was in Miami, I remember. Some circuit thing. Just me dreaming about something vague and pleasant, while Tim Baker sweat away doing my taxes and finagling breaks for me and 401K plans and all the other stupid, rather pathetic financial things he does for me, just dozing. . . . Then in my dream the calculator stopped and I began hoping, maybe this will be the night. . . .

He must have been terribly frightened, so I helped, in my sleep, undoing my belt and undoing the buttons of my jeans. Finally he came over to me.

And Kevin rushes into the room with the stuffed miniature chimp and Chester abandons his search of my body, leaps on the little chimp, hugs it. Kevin takes the page from my hand—it's a typical page like those I've seen before, continuous lines of continuous typing without a space, weird capitals and weirder punctuation, a solid rectangle of characters.

"What does it say, Chester?"

Chester nods and retrieves a red marking pen from the desk, balancing his little toy in the crook of his elbow. He takes the paper and begins to make circles on it. One by one words emerge from letters, in the circles of red ink.

"TONIE DID TIM BAKER."

Yes, I guess I did.

"TIM LOVES TONY."

And the chimp can spell my name right.

"WHEN TONY WENT HOME—"

"Oh, I can just guess what's coming," Kevin says sarcastically.

"TIM BAKER BEAT OFF CRYING."

GREENSLEEVES

It was Charlie's wife who introduced her husband to Piers—Moira Watson, who loved entertaining gay guys at their house in the Marina, at parties, dinners, impromptu gab-fests. When pressed to account for her affinity to gay men, Moira always smiled and said, "I *am* a gay man, trapped in a woman's body." You might almost believe it, so determined was her grin. "This *is* San Francisco!" she would exclaim, a sassy gleam in her large brown eyes. Moira worked for a fledgling web company with a large, dignified office, like a sliver of Tara, in the South Park section south of Market in San Francisco. VV5 designed advertising gimmicks for websites, while the money people sweated it out, hoping someone would buy some of Moira's space. Long hours, not-bad pay, lots and lots of burnout potential. And always a party to go to, many of them Moira's. Moira Watson, at 35, was always at least slightly conscious that she was old—old, that is, compared to the boys and girls who flooded Media Gulch by the thousands; the children who had been born reading William Gibson novels, netsurfing, and bobbing sleek heads to an unseen ribbon of world-rap-cyber-music; they who, therefore, had this one unimaginable advantage over her. A geometrical advantage; it was like playing Risk with an opponent who not only owns all of Asia and Europe but Mars and Venus too. Yet many of these youngsters were lazy, hadn't Moira's drive. Their posture, she figured, was what had given them the name of "slackers." When she tried to slouch, her shoulders hurt. She didn't do badly. She tried at least to keep herself from getting into an "old attitude." Gay men gave her a kind of spark; watching them and touching them she found she could still burn down the house, without drugs. Except for her Zoloft. But everyone was on Zoloft or Prozac, almost as if it weren't a drug but another form of gravity, a law to itself from which no one would want to rebel.

Afterwards, Charlie remembered the first time he saw Piers Garrison, at one of Moira's Sunday lunch parties. He'd been deputized to stand guard in the kitchen and pour margaritas. *And* keep up light chatter and pretty much play the dummy who knows nothing about computers and isn't ashamed to say so. To play Moira's husband. He would be a mirror to Moira's guests, who would receive a pleasing reflection of their own great knowledge in the silvery depths of his smiley ignorance. Naturally, since he made them feel both smart and tolerant, Moira's friends from VV5 tended to like Charlie, who worked in banking somewhere. At 43, he was way older than any of them, a man of medium height and build, with thinning fair hair and slate blue eyes. He was pouring a scotch and water, and Piers was looking up with eyes of dark green, through thick brown lashes, over the rim of the glass, and suddenly the idea hit Charlie—"Guy's got a crush on me." Then, before he could think a second thought, Moira slipped between them, slid one arm around each of their waists.

Piers Garrison was tall and lanky, well-formed, with thick wavy brown hair and fine-boned features. Charlie had to look up at him: his eyes were at the level of Piers' chin. Charlie could smell sexual excitation as well as most men, and he smelled it in the way Piers was staring at him, through sleepy-looking eyes; half-open mouth. His lips were red, as though we'd been drinking sangria, but his tongue was pale pink, like a doll's pillow.

Moira smiled. "You two don't know each other. Piers, this is my husband, Charlie Watson."

Charlie reached across Moira to shake Piers' hand. He could feel the warmth of his wife's fingertips fitted intimately inside the back of his waistband, between the suspenders. "I was making Piers a drink."

"Piers does computer graphics," she explained. "He's got the biggest Syquest drive you've ever seen."

Piers must have heard this joke a dozen times, but he grinned dutifully, though his green eyes remained thoughtful. Big white teeth on Piers for sure. Like Chiclets. What was a Syquest drive anyway?

"Hey, are you pierced?" Charlie asked, with a certain thrill of daring.

"Everyone always asks him that," said Moira, with a slight frown, "because of that name. Remember, Piers, even Vanderbilt at the meeting, and Charlie, this man Vanderbilt must be seventy, and straight as an arrow. If *he* knows about piercing, then everyone does. Another example," she began happily, "of how deeply gay male culture has penetrated the straight world, right up to the boardroom."

But Piers was blushing, furiously, as if he had never, ever, been asked the question before. He shook his head no. "Family name," he mumbled. "Nice to meet you." Moira's apartment on Chestnut boasted sensational views of the Marina—and Piers retreated, with his drink, to stand beside a full-length drape and watch the sailboats darting briskly across the purple Bay. The sun in his eyes produced a squint which wasn't, Charlie thought, unbecoming. When he wasn't squinting, Charlie thought critically, Piers' looks were kind of bland. It was when he was in pain that they took on the noble pallor of, say, Peter O'Toole in *Lawrence of Arabia.* He wondered what kind of underwear Piers had on—right now. Like a flip book of paper dolls, he pictured Piers in different kinds of underwear, standing against a perfectly blank background he could cut away at will with a pair of sharp scissors. Decided he looked best in boxer shorts—white ones like his own, perhaps with tiny shamrocks dotting them to match his eyes. Whether Piers actually wore them or not was an open question.

But he wasn't pierced—*if* he were telling the truth, and Charlie prided himself on his ability to spot a liar at thirty paces.

One afternoon a few days later Charlie called his wife's office and asked the receptionist to connect him to Piers. "Remember me?"

"Yes, sir, I sure do," said Piers.

"I was thinking maybe you and I should get together."

For a few seconds Charlie could hear nothing on the other end of the line. He was about to hang up, when he heard Piers' voice again. "Sir, you're right."

"What's your address?"

Piers gave it to him.

"What kind of underwear you got on, right now?"

The slight pause before Piers replied was all Charlie needed to know. It was the slight pause of the man who, though not a *habitual* liar, is anxious to cater to the erotic fantasies of another, more manly man. They made a date for that evening.

"I guess I'm at a time in my life when I need a change," Charlie confided, over a mountain of beef at the House of Prime Rib at Van Ness. Its baronial atmosphere, its smoky smells of overcooked spinach and beef, and big tankers of beer, were a little out of Piers' element, which is where Charlie wanted him. Off-kilter, he thought, confusing this tired metaphor with a mental image of a kilt; a kilt drawn up over the lower parts of a naked Scots guardsman. Off-kilter. "You have family here in the City?"

"I have a brother," Piers said slowly. "He's gay too."

"Ever have sex with him?"

Piers looked shocked, but Charlie persisted. "Why not, what's wrong with me asking you that?"

"Eddy's a whole lot younger than I am," responded Piers, slowly, distracted and troubled. By this time Charlie had the tongs from the salad in Piers' lap, and was rubbing up and down his dick like a violin. "He's twenty, I'm twenty-nine."

"Well, I want to meet him," Charlie said. "Sometime." He added that Piers could be his sub if he wanted to, and Piers agreed—this radiant smile broke across his face like the sun breaking free of fog. Charlie didn't expect such instant compliance. It knocked him on his ass.

Piers lived in a cottage, set back from the street, just about in the backyard of another house, in a part of San Francisco some call "Glen Park." This is where he received Charlie, where he wrote a contract at a big mahogany desk in which he swore to serve Charlie for the rest of his life. Signed it with blood. They both did. Charlie liked to do a lot of reading, so early on he told Piers that if he ever wanted to express himself, it must be in writing. "Dear Sir, may I suck your cock?" "Please sir, whip my white bitch ass with your thick brown money belt." Simple things. Little love notes. "I don't want to hear a word out of your mouth," Charlie said. "I get enough yakking at home."

He pointed to Piers' computer. "Type me some notes on that," he said. "Tell me about what I should do to your skinny butt." While Piers was typing, very nimbly, Charlie picked up a framed photo from Piers' mantelpiece. This was "Eddy," Pier's young brother, who was twenty and what Piers described as a "club kid." Charlie hardly knew what that was, but suspected the worst. Eddy's sullen gaze and full lower lip turned Charlie on. He'd like to have half an hour making that lower lip quiver. He wondered if Eddy was a bottom too. He looked more fleshy than Piers, whose body was rather, I don't know, aesthetic.

One evening Charlie spotted an empty crushed beer can sitting in the garbage can Piers kept chained to one side of the cottage. "You don't drink beer," Charlie said. "What the fuck is this, pal?"

"Dear Sir," Piers wrote, "the can of beer belonged to the FedEx man who asked me if he could dispose of it." Doesn't that sound like a lie? The long steady gaze he wore gravely on his beautiful face was like a dare in three dimensions. Is he taunting me? With this beer can, of all things? They watched Charlie's hand crunch the thing to a flat shiny surface. They watched the thing pierce the soft skin or web between his thumb and forefinger. They watched the two drops of blood flood to the surface, and Charlie, at least, thought he saw a vindicated sort of pleasure in Piers' steady gaze.

Charlie was the lazy kind of top who makes his slave do all the talking. Why not, it was tiring working at his office, the gym was fatiguing, Moira never stopped planning her career. "Continue!" became his favorite word, as Piers typed out story after story, like Scheherezade. Part of the fun was watching him try to entertain his master with words, since he wasn't a verbal guy to begin with, but Charlie educated him as best as he could. Soon Piers was spouting off like a regular blue whale scribbling these Balzacian tales of the sex marketplace while Charlie watched TV or just relaxed. Before Charlie's arrival, Piers would ascertain what he wanted to eat or drink while visiting, and he kept his VCR supplied with a steady stream of videos, porn and others. At Piers' job he often had access to tapes of first-run movies that were still playing the expensive theaters. "I like Stallone," Charlie told Piers. "He's an amazing physical specimen and they say he's no dummy." So, every time Sly makes a new picture I want to see it. None of that waiting on line shit. Not for Charlie Watson." Meanwhile Piers was on the floor, writing away in the notebook of questions or typing Charlie some sentences about having to love having to be his slave. Charlie made him write so fast his sentences had no beginning or end. "I like to be fucked My ass is so tight, 'cause never have REAL sex. Ok. I used some big sticks sometimes, even the U-lock of bike. Please do it. fuck me hard Thank you, sir!!! I'd like to do whatever you wanna me to do. Yes, sir. Thank you! I'm daddy's boy now, aren't I, Charlie? Yes, I am. Piers says, I feel proud to be your son. I belongs to CHARLIE!"

Charlie: "Tell me, Piers. Louder."

Piers: "CHARLIE!!! CHARLIE!!! No, you can abuse my ass anytime you want. Please use my ass. Charlie, sir, you'll just tell me drop my pants. And then spread my 2 cheeks. And Piers will do what you want with your boy I belong to you." Charlie told him to act out his desires, whatever they were, and Piers stood on tiptoe in his own bedroom, reached for the ceiling with one hand, and with the other felt for his own cock and pulled it out to its furthest extension. A white-label dance music compilation chugged onto the stereo, some emo-boy Cleveland sobber. Charlie laughed as Piers jerked himself off, since his body was so awkward, so willing to please. He was wearing the pair of boxer shorts Charlie made him wear all the time, white with tiny green shamrocks, and his dick stuck out of it ragged, hard and somehow still prim. His thighs were trembling under the burden of such unwavering sensuality. He concentrated on the music to take his mind off the orgasm he wanted to unleash. The unknown track that had opened the compilation had moved into the Brothers in Rhythm mix of Kylie's "Too Far." Piers acknowledged the relevance of the darkly poetic track on the moment in hand. Charlie wasn't really listening, he lay sprawled on the bed examining this picture—words suddenly made flesh.

Over Piers' mind and body Charlie had, contractually, every right but one—he had not the right to ask why Piers was doing this. Nor why Piers loved him.

One Saturday afternoon Charlie was at home flipping through *TV Guide* while Moira was on the phone in the next room, giggling. After she hung up, she said, "That was Piers. The one with the green eyes I'm sure you don't remember." Moira had convinced herself that Charlie never paid attention to any of her colleagues and pals, that to Charlie all the "gay guys" she brought home were more or less indistinguishable. And they were, to a certain extent. So why was Charlie annoyed to hear Moira laughing with Piers?

"We were talking about the magnetic door at Farjeon."

"Magnetic door?" Charlie said with a frown.

Moira blushed. Or she would have, if she hadn't told the story so often—to others. "It was at Farjeon—I'm sure I told you this story already,"

"Believe me, you didn't."

"It's silly. But anyhow at Farjeon there's this anti-static room with a magnetic door, and Piers and I were there one day when this boy, this temp, this wonderful red-headed punk boy, got swept right into the door and was pinned there. As though a strong hurricane were pressing him into the door. He could barely breathe. Security had to come and turn off the EM."

"For God's sake, why?"

Evidently this was something multimedia people understood instinctively. "It was a demo magnetic door, and he—this boy—had been caught there by his piercings. I think one or two must have come out. It must have been terribly painful, I know they brought him to St. Luke's right afterward."

Charlie picked up the magazine and continued to read the story on *Star Trek,* disgruntled. "Your friends are disgusting," he said.

Finally the evening came when, as Charlie requested, Eddy, Piers' younger brother, came to pay a call. "Tell your brother who you belong to," Charlie suggested, while the three of them sat in the kitchen drinking brandy after dinner.

"I belong to Charlie," Piers said, bitterly ashamed at being so abased in front of his younger, skeptical bro. As it turned out, Eddy was intrigued at the setup. He offered to have sex with Charlie as well. "Compare how I do it, with how he does it," he said witheringly. "Piers hasn't even got a dick, far as I'm concerned."

But Eddy wasn't exactly a bottom and wanted to run things his way. Charlie grunted and the two of them went upstairs to Piers' bedroom, where Charlie ordered Piers to tie himself to a chair and watch. Eddy Garrison had none of Piers' weird angularity; his body was more compact, chunkier. Eddy's hair was the color of butter, with cocoa trailed in, and his chest and butt were sculpted out of some marvelous soft marble, you wanted to eat food from them, and in due course Charlie did. Piers' eyes were the fresh color of moss, a soft bright green, filled with an open frank awareness of the world. but whereas you might have said that he was the more sensitive of the two brothers, you wanted to fuck Eddy up more.

Charlie put his hands on Eddy's shoulders and kept up the pressure, increasing until Eddy squatted between his knees. Sulkily the boy began to suck Charlie's cock, lopped his mouth round it as though nursing. His eyes rolled, disgruntled and not amused, in their deep sockets. Charlie had to cuff him a little to get him into line. Piers looked on, expressionless, tho' Charlie did his best to include him in the conversation.

"Your brother's a good cocksucker," he said suggestively, tho' Eddy wasn't, not really.

Eddy was the younger brother Piers always felt responsible for, always told him to take condoms with him wherever he went, tried to discourage him from hard drugs, etc. Wished he would go back to college. It embarrassed Piers to know that Eddy was abreast of his own situation but, he thought, "I asked for it." When Charlie finally came, Piers winced as Eddy swallowed part of his semen, then dribbled the rest onto Charlie's big hairy legs.

"You two are regular sex pigs, ain't you?" Eddy guessed. "Look, guys, have fun, I'm off to a party."

After he had sashayed out there was a certain tension, while Charlie questioned Piers about Eddy's sex life. He was certain—absolutely certain—that Eddy sneaked over while Piers was alone. Frantically Piers typed out, "No sir I never fucked Eddy, he's my own brother no sir I am true to you."

"Fuck you," Charlie snapped. The following week he lowered Piers onto the burner in the kitchen range as it glowed with the slightest tinge of orange. "This is for being your brother's little sex wimp," he said, as he held Piers in his arms and gently pressed his left asscheek onto the lit burner and held it there until they could both smell the flesh burning. Charlie compared the way Piers scrambled in his arms to trying to bathe a cat. Then, a week later, he gave the same treatment to Piers' right cheek. Now Piers' ass bore two sets of spiral branding marks, brown, crackly thin flesh like pork rinds—like a strip of pork rind laid into circles on each half of his slim white butt. Piers said he didn't feel the marks, except a little in bad weather, when they creaked, but to the touch they were certainly different than the rest of that naked flesh—they were like brownish ribbon interwoven on the front of a Hallmark card, silky, as a bookbinder might underlay calfskin with Victorian ribbon. Charlie liked the look, but Eddy groaned when he saw it. "Tacky!" he hooted. "Next he'll cook you, bro." Eddy and Charlie had Piers bend over his couch so they could examine his butt. Eddy ran his be-ringed fingers over the punctured skin, lingered a little at the crack, giggled at Charlie. Piers started to cry, but stopped after a minute when Charlie ordered him to. As Charlie and Eddy pointed out, he was hard as a rock through the whole examination. "Almost looks like Piers has a dick," Eddy hooted.

"Charlie," said his wife, "know what's funny? Piers Garrison has been so quiet and withdrawn at the office. Almost mopey. He used to be so much fun. Do you think he's sick?" She always said "sick" when she meant AIDS. Charlie shrugged, left it at that.

"Call him," he said. "Now which one was he?"

"The real cute one with the brown hair, like Cindy Crawford with a butch haircut, but you wouldn't remember."

Charlie told Piers to place a personals ad in the paper offering to fuck strangers under his master's supervision. In this way Charlie made many new pals who would come over to Glen Park to fuck Piers; all exclaimed at the perfection of this decorated ass. There were regular party nights, and Piers realized these were Charlie's way of counterposing Moira's festive cocktail parties with some fun of his own. Late one Thursday night he stood in a corner on his house, naked but for his dirty shamrock underwear, watching some men fighting over the last pieces of Leon's Barbeque left on his kitchen table. Others were sitting watching a tape of *Friends* on TV and arguing about whether Matt LeBlanc were gay or not, while three bottles of champagne sat in the open refrigerator. Others sat at card tables spread with brown paper, drinking Diet Cokes and coffee and eating sugar doughnuts. Piers looked at them all for a minute. Then he went upstairs to his bedroom. It hurt him a little to climb. The wooden stairs creaked under his feet. The men who watched him saw the dirt on the soles of his white crew socks.

"I have a new boyfriend," Charlie said to Piers. "Young boy, studious, who I met at the Hole in the Wall. He was dancing on top of the bar in his jockey shorts."

"Maybe you'll bring him by, Charlie?"

Piers sat at Charlie's feet, with a tiny knife, scraping the peels from potatoes a bushel of potatoes, one by one, in a very dim light.

"I don't know if I want you to meet him," he told Piers. "He's a very innocent boy, not a jaded roué like you. Morals infect the young. Once he rubs against you, he'll have this stain on him, gray and sour, like the inside of an old ashtray."

"Yes, you're probably right," said Piers. The peeler slipped out of his hand and clinked a mournful sound on the tile floor. "I'm clumsy today."

"Clumsy and ugly."

"I am ugly," said Piers, looking at his dusty hands, which smelled like potatoes. Later when he had peeled enough potatoes, then fried and sautéed them, Charlie was going to make him eat them all, then hold them down.

"Know what my new boyfriend's name is? Eddy Garrison."

Piers went to the keyboard of the glowing PC. "Dear Sir," he began.

"I want those potatoes peeled," Charlie growled. "Get your hands away from that computer." And Piers complied.

Eddy liked to prance around Piers' apartment in a leather vest and pink garters decorated with roses. His bottom bare. He knew it was a pert one. It looked like someone had dashed a bowl of milk over a pair of bowling balls. "Charlie and I are going to the opera," Eddy told Piers, his eyes wide, when the two brothers were alone one evening. "Imagine, me at the opera, with all those opera queens. An opera lasts for hours, and hours. And you'll be here, tucking yourself in like a good boy. Piers, I saw a mother putting her kid in a car seat, buckled him in, tucked his ears under this little wool cap, and I thought of you, bro! Don't know why . . . just did."

"I belong to him," Piers said, more or less steadily. "Don't know why, but I do."

"Know what me and Charlie call you, Piers? We call you 'Email,' cause you have those circa brands on your ass."

"Oh really?"

"Yeah, we laugh about it when we're out at the opera, Piers! 'Wonder how ol' Email's doing tonight.' 'He's flat on his stomach for sure.'" Eddy paused, taking a drag off a big purple joint. He studied his older brother's weary silence. "You don't have to put up with this shit, bro. How much fun can it be for you, all these Hispanic dudes and old geezers traipsing up here to fuck you while some others hold you down."

"You put a washcloth in my mouth," Piers said flatly. "And it was soaked with cum."

"To shut you up, bro," said Eddy, stubbing the joint in an ashtray. "You were hollering so loud I thought the neighbors would call in the cops." He lowered himself onto the bed next to Piers, and sniffed. "That old pair of drawers smells, you know that? It stinks, why doesn't he let you wash it?" He took Piers' hand and placed it firmly on his own pierced cock, rubbed the limp resisting hand over his cock until it grew hard, rose from his body like a wand.

"I remember when you were little," Piers said, looking away from Eddy's erection. "Back in Austin I used to take you to Sunday school."

"Well those were the days," Eddy replied. "Now pretend I'm Charlie Watson, lick my big fat dick, bro, make it happen."

"No thanks," said Piers, rolling away from Eddy. He remembered bringing Eddy to church, holding his hand when Eddy was eight or nine, sharing a hymnbook with him, tho' it seemed clear even then that Eddy was no reader. In those days it was easy to mistake Eddy's clear amused gaze for the insouciance of the innocent. He would give Eddy a dollar to put in the collection plate.

After he left, Piers walked to his front window, watched Eddy saunter down the steps to his bike. Eddy waved insouciantly, winked.

"Please, Charlie, just leave Eddy out of this. I don't care what you do to me, just leave him alone."

"You don't have it in your head, do you, pal? I'll do what I like with whomever I please, and to tell you the truth, that includes your brother for sure."

Piers remembered Eddy putting the crumpled dollar bill into the jingling collection plate, the pride and satisfaction on his round face. "Dear Charlie," he thought. He kept composing these long letters to Charlie, not writing them out, just writing them in his head, seeing them written out along the pale bedsheets in the moonlight. Alphabets of disjointed desire that would never see the light of day. His arms itched to type them up. But he was afraid to. "Sir, I would not complain to you for myself, but I hope that you will spare my brother some of your harder caresses, for he was reared differently than me, and he is a softer boy, his pain threshold lower than mine. If you seek to punish him, withhold your punishment from him, give it to me instead.

"Instead pamper him like a baby, because he understands no better than a baby does."

One Sunday when Charlie came to Glen Park, Piers was not present. Charlie let himself in with his own key, at the kitchen door, and padded to the refrigerator for champagne. From the CD player floated the tune of an old Elizabethan madrigal, sung by one of those countertenors Moira adored. "Greensleeves," Charlie whispered, the big bottle of Veuve Clicquot Ponsardin halfway to his lips. "Alas, my love, you do me wrong to cast me off discourteously; for I have lovèd you so long, delighting in your company." The phone rang and Charlie answered it. Moira was calling. "Eddy Garrison called me," she began. "He told me the whole sad story."

Charlie stared at the phone, then noticed the general emptiness of the cottage. The CD player stood on the mantelpiece, where once Eddy's framed photo had stood. The chairs, the sofa, even the rugs were gone.

Moira continued, in a sort of drone. With part of his mind, Charlie thought, *she must be doing twice her goddam Zoloft.* "Eddy knew just where you would be and how you'd answer the phone." Piers' big computer was gone, and his Syquest drive, his printer. The desk they once sat on—gone. All his pictures, the walls were bare. "Eddy told me how if I called, you'd pick up for sure, thinking it was some respondent to your lovely personal ad. But it's not, Charlie—not this time. In case you're curious, Eddy's taken Piers back to Texas with him."

"Who is this?" Charlie whispered hoarsely.

"Someone you've done wrong," Moira said, before slipping the phone back on the receiver.

In the trash bin in the kitchen he found half a dozen empty champagne bottles, and the stained shamrock boxers. With a sick shuddering sigh Charlie fell against the wall, pinching his face with his hands. The CD voice continued, mocking him, like the Emperor's nightingale, exquisite, heartbreaking. "For I have lovèd you so long, delighting in your company."

Poet, novelist, critic, playwright, and original member of the "New Narrative" group, Kevin Killian has written a book of poetry, *Argento Series* (2001); three novels, *Shy* (1989), *Arctic Summer* (1997), and *Spreadeagle* (2010); a book of memoirs, *Bedrooms Have Windows* (1989); and a book of stories, *Little Men* (1996), that won the PEN Oakland award for fiction. A second collection, *I Cry Like a Baby*, was published by Painted Leaf Books in 2001. With Lew Ellingham, Killian has written the biography of Jack Spicer, *Poet Be Like God* (1998), and co-edited Spicer's posthumous books *The Train of Thought* (1994) and *The Tower of Babel* (1994). With Peter Gizzi, he co-edited *My Vocabulary Did This to Me: The Collected Poems of Jack Spicer* (2008). Killian's work has been widely anthologized and has appeared in, among others, *Best American Poetry 1988* (ed. John Ashbery), and *Discontents* (ed. Dennis Cooper). His newest books are a book of *Selected Amazon Reviews* (2006) and a book of poems dedicated to Kylie Minogue, *Action Kylie* (2008).

For the San Francisco Poets Theater, Killian has written thirty plays, including *Stone Marmalade* (1996, with Leslie Scalapino), *The American Objectivists* (2001, with Brian Kim Stefans), and *Often* (also 2001, with Barbara Guest). With Dodie Bellamy, he has edited 154 issues of the SF-based writing/art zine they call "Mirage #4/Period(ical)."